A MAN
IN DARKNESS

FINDING COURAGE TO FORGIVE

Foster Nash

A Man in Darkness
Finding Courage to Forgive
Foster Nash © 2022

ISBN: 978-1-61206-286-0

Published by

ALOHA
PUBLISHING

Printed in the United States of America

DEDICATION

This book is dedicated to Frederick Simmons and George Frederick Whaley.

My father-in-law, **Fred Simmons** (March 1936 – Dec 2021) passed away last year and left a big hole in our lives. He was a man of honor and love. Like a ship's wake, Dad's heading was true, he knew that God was his compass to his way home. His wake was wide, the love for his family and friends ran deep. His wake was strong, he led by example, stood tall and strong. And his path ahead was always at full speed, he knew where he was heading. God's speed, Fred Simmons.

George Whaley (Born Feb 28, 2022) is Fred's latest great-grandson and is new to this world. As you, dear reader, read these words, George is creating a wake of his own, beginning his course through life. We pray for George every day, for his grace, and his salvation. I pray he lives with the honor and strength of his grandfather and that he will stand tall and make his Lord, his parents, and his family proud. God's speed, George Whaley. May your course be true. May you grow up to be a strong man, a kind man.

CONTENTS

PROLOGUE

4 AD

TUSCANY

It was close to sunset when Cassius raced through his father's wheat fields, running as fast as his eight-year-old legs could manage in the ankle-deep mud. Despite yesterday's rain and running between three-foot rows of harvestable wheat, Cassius's thin legs were able to keep up the pursuit even though he felt as though his leather sandals were being pulled down into the mud with each step. Lifting each leg out of the thick slop as fast as he could, with a squelch and grunt, he worked to keep his focus on his moving target.

"Bracus, run faster. He's outrunning us!" Cassius screamed while trying to suck in as much air as his lungs could manage. Bracus, his best friend from birth, was having better success negotiating the mud with his shorter but stronger legs.

Just ahead of both, Max, the family dog, stopped and looked back to watch his pursuers struggle through the wheat fields. Wagging his muddy tail, he took off again, loving the chase-me game.

The frantic chase continued in the muddied wheat field. Ahead of him and to the right, Cassius watched as Bracus suddenly tripped in ankle-deep mud, landing face first. Bracus jumped up and continued to run while wiping muddied water from his eyes. As Cassius passed him on the left, Bracus turned toward Cassius and saw him point toward a gully that would allow Bracus to shortcut the path to Max.

Meanwhile, Max ran hard, holding tightly to the stolen prize between his teeth, a statue highly valued by both boys. Despite the inherent advantage of Max's stability, having four legs to plow through the mud and canine reflexes, Cassius was slowly gaining on him out of sheer desperation, pushing his legs as fast as they could run.

Cassius continued the pounding pace and worked to push Max toward the gully while keeping an eye on Bracus angling closer toward Max on his right. Turning to see Bracus, Max hesitated as Cassius leaped onto Max's hindquarters and wrestled the dog into the mud. Wrapping the dog firmly in his arms, Cassius tried to free the statue from the dog's jaws. Eventually, with the help of Bracus, both boys were able to open Max's jaws enough to take the statue of Epona from the dog's death grip.

Looking down on the broken wooden horse, Cassius's worst fears were realized. Panting heavily, Max returned his stare with a look of innocence. Wagging his tail, he jumped free and took off in the direction of the house. Frustrated and hurt, Cassius wanted to kick his dog as he ran away, but instantly knew better. He was responsible for carelessly leaving the statute of Epona on the table of the farmhouse. His father's lessons about finding the truth and taking responsibility had been burned deep within his eight-year-old mind.

Cassius turned away from Bracus and sat down in the mud, defeated. Wiping the sweat from his brow and the tears from his eyes, he looked at the retreating dog. The sun was setting in a brilliant purple sky behind the farmhouse. On any other day, Cassius would have stopped to watch the colors shifting in the sky near the horizon, but today it was a difficult reminder of precious things lost.

Cassius cradled the broken parts of the statue as they headed home, Bracus close to his side. Both boys walked in silence, there was no need to express the hurt Cassius felt. Reaching the small farmhouse as dusk fell, Cassius's father took the statute and held the broken pieces in his calloused hands. Looking down at Cassius, and then at Bracus, his father's eyes were sympathetic as he shook his head.

"If Papa were here, we could make this whole again, son. But Papa is gone. We all miss him." Quintus Dias put a hand on his son's head, and the other on Bracus. "It's harvest season and the rains came early this year. I'll try to fix it for you after the Equus October, boys."

Quintus Dias stood for a moment, just looking at Cassius with the love of a father that could not resolve his son's pain. Quintus knew that Epona wasn't just a wooden horse, it was the boy's idea of a deity that provided him hope and a future beyond the daily grind of farm life.

What made Epona even more special, was that Cassius's grandfather, whom he called Papa, had hand carved Epona, the horse statue, the year before he passed. Both Cassius and Bracus loved Papa and the quiet evenings filled with stories of ancient heroes and gods, him telling the boys about their history, and explaining their spiritual heritage. For Cassius and Bracus, Papa wasn't just an old man, he was the repository of knowledge, hope, adventure, and love. And through the bonds with Papa, Bracus became not just a friend, but more of a true brother to Cassius.

For the two years since Papa had lovingly created the statue, Cassius and Bracus had lit candles and prayed to Epona, both for luck and good fortune. There was a simple beauty in the carved wooden figure. Cassius admired its graceful lines almost as much as he admired the effortless dignity of horses as they grazed and ran through the fields. With tails in the air and flowing manes, the grace horses showed while running at a full gallop always took the boys' breath away. Both Cassius and Bracus believed horses reflected their own desires for unbridled freedom. The boys and the horses were kindred spirits from different species. As part of their equine spirits, Cassius and Bracus took every opportunity to gallop the family horses through the country roads, riding the winds of boyhood. Along those paths, they discovered adventures and purpose as they played the parts of Roman cavalrymen, like their fathers, fighting in distant wars and conquering strange new worlds. Cassius and Bracus had vowed to each other, one day they would be real Roman soldiers.

"I'll need your help in the fields starting tomorrow, son. Bracus, your dad will likely need you too. If we don't harvest this wheat immediately, now that it's rained, we'll lose everything. Wash your hands for supper. A full bath to clean off the mud will have to wait." Cassius looked into his father's eyes and saw worry. The rain had surprised his father.

Cassius stood back as his father went to wash for supper, fighting back tears of regret and loss. Cassius knew wooden statutes could be fixed, but the summer's wheat could not be allowed to die in the field. Bracus looked over and nudged Cassius. "Your dad will fix it after the harvest. He always keeps his promises."

4 AD

MAGDALA, GALILEE

The Roman sergeant approached the courtyard doorway of the mud-brick home, raised his right foot, and kicked the wooded door open. "Now!" he screamed.

Inside, the twelve, armed Jewish Zealots stiffened, then grabbed their weapons in response to the break-in. Joseph reacted first.

"Move, Matthias!" Joseph yelled as he saw the Roman archer move into the courtyard doorway, taking aim. The arrow released just as Joseph shoved Matthias aside, pushing him to the ground.

Joseph screamed. "Arrrrgh!" The archer's arrow had pierced his leather breastplate, pushing the broadhead tip into his shoulder.

Scrabbling up from the floor, Matthias watched his best friend slump to the ground against the back wall. Matthias turned and yelled to his fellow Zealot soldiers who had already started scattering throughout the small home. "Roman soldiers! Out the back door, archers to the side windows!"

A dozen men scrambled to escape what was once their sanctuary, but now had become their entrapment, as Roman soldiers began to move around the courtyard trying to encircle the home.

Matthias picked up a javelin, arched his back, and turning his right shoulder, he launched the spear toward the Roman archer, who was now moving into the courtyard. A second later, the spear struck the center of the archer's breastplate. Mortally wounded, the archer stumbled back to the courtyard doorway, blocking the entrance. Sergeant Orestes caught him as he fell, looking down as his friend of ten years, died in his arms.

Sergeant Orestes screamed in agony, ordering his soldiers, "Get that man!"

Back in the house, Matthias looked down on Joseph, broke the shaft off the arrow lodged into his shoulder, and then lifted him by his other shoulder. Arm in arm, the pair started a broken run through the house.

Just as Matthias had trained his men, two armed Zealots jumped out of each side window to establish a defensive position against the Roman encirclement of the house. Their orders were to shoot two arrows to slow down the Romans, then fall back to join their companions. Matthias gave a small sigh of relief as he saw the plan executed flawlessly, giving the remaining eight occupants time to escape. The Zealots then scattered to pre-determined safe houses.

Sergeant Orestes stood in front of the home and saw the Zealots scatter. He hesitated as his men ducked arrows that were shot by Zealots from the sides of the house. After five minutes of waiting for the rest of his soldiers to arrive, the sergeant ordered his men into four-man search parties. "Go house to house but be careful of ambushes!" he shouted.

Meanwhile, running through the back alleys of Magdala, Matthias took off his tunic to wrap around Joseph's wound, trying to hide the broken arrow and blood running down his breastplate. Moving as fast as Joseph could manage, they turned several corners of the narrow, cobbled streets of Magdala, trying to lose any pursuers. Finally, a woman with long, black, braided hair waved them into a nearby home.

"Susanna, Joseph's hurt!" Matthias announced as he pulled off his tunic, exposing the broken arrow lodged in Joseph's shoulder. "He saved my life!"

Susanna immediately laid Joseph on the table, pulled off his breastplate, and examined the wound. "It's bad, but he'll live. The breastplate kept it from going too deep."

Susanna called for Rachel from the back to help. "This is Rachel, she'll help us with Joseph. She's a good friend, who owns this house with her husband, Achi, and daughter Mary."

"Achi is fishing," explained Rachel, holding her new baby Mary, as she walked into the room.

"Rachel, this is my brother, Matthias."

Matthias nodded in acknowledgment as he helped pull Joseph's clothes away from his shoulder.

Susanna made two quick incisions and then pulled the arrow out from Joseph's shoulder while Matthias held his still body. Fortunately, Joseph had passed out as they removed the arrow and could not complain about the pain.

"Quick, we must move him underneath the house. Soldiers will be searching house-to-house for us. I'll leave from the back door to another location," Matthias ordered.

As soon as Susanna had bandaged and wrapped the wound, Rachel left to a back room and removed a rug and several floorboards, leaving an opening to a large root cellar. Matthias and Susanna wrapped Joseph in a blanket and the three carefully lowered him into the cellar with Matthias taking his weight while climbing down the precarious ladder.

As they lifted Joseph down, he groaned in pain. "He's awake Matthias, I'll stay with him and keep him quiet." Matthias nodded his approval to Susanna, made sure that Joseph was comfortable in the blankets, and quietly and quickly climbed the ladder to leave the house.

The room fell into darkness as quiet thuds and scrapes indicated that the floorboards and mats had been returned to their original position, making the root cellar hidden once again.

"Where am I?" Joseph asked in a choked whisper as dust descended through the gaps in the floorboards overhead.

"Shhh, Joseph . . . you're in a friend's house, in the root cellar. You're hurt. Matthias brought you here. We need to be quiet, Roman soldiers are searching for you and Matthias," answered Susanna as she adjusted the folded blanket under his head

"Matthias?" asked Joseph as he looked around the darkened root cellar.

"He went to find his other men. Try not to move, I haven't stitched your wound yet."

"Susanna . . ." Joseph looked up to see the worry on her face. "This was my last Zealot raid. I had just told Matthias that Sara and I are engaged, that I wanted to settle down, be a husband and a father." As he mentioned Sara, Joseph's eyes began to tear up.

"Matthias is your best friend, Joseph. He will understand." Susanna reached for his hand.

"But . . . I know our independence is important to Matthias. He's a good leader and a godly rabbi. No one else could train us how to fight so well." Joseph paused to breathe.

"If Sara weren't in my life, it would be different. I'd fight for Matthias to the death. But she is my betrothed, I can't leave her now." Tears leaked from Joseph's eyes and disappeared in the hair at his temples.

"Shhhh . . . I think soldiers are coming," whispered Susanna.

9 AD
NAZARETH, GALILEE

Eithen threw a rock that struck Yeshua on the right thigh. "You're a mama's boy! Maybe because you don't know your father!" He laughed. The rumors in Nazareth had always been there, but as the boys grew, they began to understand the consequences of rumors about Yeshua being conceived out of wedlock.

Yeshua looked around at the twelve boys in the olive grove. Most were looking at him, some were smirking, others were laughing at his pain, but a few were keeping silent in the background.

Yeshua could only look around in anguish, the insults penetrating deep. '*I know my Father!*' he screamed inside.

The rock that struck him had only left a minor laceration; the real wound was to his heart. It was obvious he was pained, his eyes wet, yet he stood silent.

He knew these boys; they had been his friends for most of their lives. '*How could they attack me? I haven't changed, I haven't hurt them.*'

'You're so perfect Yeshua, you don't even have the courage to steal bread from the baker. You're a mama's boy!" Eithen shouted again.

'*I am different,*' Yeshua admitted to himself.

Despite their cruelty, Yeshua calmed himself and paused. His shoulders dropped slightly as he forced his anxieties to leave. Understanding he was different, he accepted the fact that he would always be different. Not only was it ok, but it was good.

Instead of fighting back, Yeshua looked up, scrutinizing each boy standing in front of him. Slowly he looked into their eyes, one by one. His message was clear. He knew each one of them and they knew him. Slowly, he connected with each boy, offering forgiveness through a look, a word, or a nod.

One by one the taunting stopped, until all that could be heard was the bleating of goats in the nearby field. The boys understood. Two of the boys turned and walked away, consumed with guilt and angry that their taunting had failed. Two other boys were so shaken by his reaction, they silently cried on their way home, their malicious spirits broken.

It was Eithen alone who squinted his eyes, as though he was looking directly into the sun, then ground his teeth and snarled. The remaining boys just stood silent, not wanting to move. They were frozen by the unexpected gracious response.

On that early morning in an olive grove just east of Nazareth, Yeshua gave them a gift they had not expected, nor were ready to understand. Yeshua showed them the strength of forgiveness. Yeshua had the courage to forgive, despite his own pain.

Chapter 1

HIDDEN TREASURES

16 AD
THE TEMPLE

Nicodemus looked up at Joseph Caiaphas and grimaced. *'Of all the Pharisees to select from the court of the Sanhedrin, they had to choose Caiaphas to be my mentor. He is the most grating of all the Pharisees, and the least trustworthy,'* he thought to himself.

Walking through the still-dark streets of Jerusalem to the Temple on the eastern side of the city, Nicodemus moved as fast as he could without running. *'I waited for you for an hour and now you hurry?'* Nicodemus was frustrated.

It was just past sunrise when they entered the outer steps of the Temple, walking across the Gentiles' Courtyard toward the massive Temple sanctuary. As the sun eclipsed the white stone walls of Fortress Antonia, Nicodemus shaded his eyes from the brightness.

Joseph broke into a run once they reached the stairs just below the massive entrance, Nicodemus staying three steps behind him. As Nicodemus scurried through the Temple's magnificent gate, he looked up to see the 40-foot columns towering over him. The sun's glaring reflection blinded him briefly as it shone off the brass overlay on the base of the columns.

Blinking to clear his vision, another flash of light came suddenly from the eastern portal of the towering walls of Fortress Antonia. Nicodemus momentarily hesitated, distracted by the burst of brilliant light, like arrows shooting past the fortress silhouette. Looking upward again, he identified another smaller flash; sunlight reflecting off the helmet of a Roman soldier. Nicodemus wondered why the officer stood alone, in full battle dress, his ruby plume fluttering in the breeze. He released an involuntary shutter, nearly stumbling on the Temple steps as he moved toward the gates.

"Let's move, Nicodemus!" Caiaphas barked from the gates, 10 yards ahead. "We have a lot to do this morning." Nicodemus begrudgingly obeyed Joseph, his newly appointed 'mentor' in the Sanhedrin. He refocused on their morning's task and quickened his pace across the Women's Courtyard.

Looking around as they raced through the Women's Courtyard, Nicodemus was amazed at how clean the courtyard was kept, despite the daily traffic of people crowding the Temple. Levites worked each night to keep the courtyard swept and polished. Even this early, merchants were already gathering along with money changers, tax collectors, and offering booths for widows and the poor.

As Nicodemus and Joseph approached the circular twelve-step stairway of the Nicanor Gate, the entrance to the Priests' Courtyard, he looked to his right and saw that the Levite choirs were preparing to sing a chorus of Psalms.

"That's odd this early in the morning," commented Nicodemus.

Joseph turned to him. "I directed them to begin early today. It's a distraction. Move faster, you're slowing us down. We need to finish our business in the Temple before the crowds come."

Nicodemus knew better than to follow up with more questions. This alone reaffirmed his experience with Joseph Caiaphas. Joseph was shrewd. He loved directing people in plans he rarely shared.

"I never could trust Caiaphas," Nicodemus reflected on the man he had known since childhood. *'He's always trying to find fault in other people. And his disdain for the common Jew has grown since becoming a Pharisee. It seems he believes God's people were placed here to serve him . . . to make him look good or gain more power."*

While the previous Women's Courtyard was clean but rather plain, the Priests' Courtyard was immaculate—polished floors, ornate rugs, and drapes woven with rich gold and silver threads hanging in the inner colonnades. Nicodemus carefully walked across the expansive courtyard surrounded by colonnades and apartments . . . hesitant to disturb the richness of the Priests' court.

Despite the summer's daily heat, he trembled as he crossed the Temple stones. *'They are as cold as a witch's heart.'* Every time he crossed the Temple floor, it reminded him that God's Spirit had left the Temple over 600 years ago, just before King Nebuchadnezzar destroyed the Temple in 586 BC.

"We've disappointed our God so many times," he whispered.

Despite the Temple's overwhelming courtyards, sacrificial altars, and cleansing pool, Nicodemus could not feel a spiritual presence. He had heard the rumors that the Ark of the Covenant had never been returned to the Temple since the previous Temple's destruction. Nevertheless, the daily routines of priests and Pharisees kept up the appearance that the Jews still maintained an active covenant with their God.

As he hurried across the middle of the Priests Courtyard, past the huge sacrificial altar and the giant Laver Pool, Nicodemus looked up at the 15-foot-tall altar. He realized the monuments stood as symbols of the Hebrews themselves. Sacrifice and cleansing were integral to Jewish life and history, a ritual that constantly ingrained their need for spiritual renewal.

Nicodemus stopped to look up past the altars. The sun crowned the upper part of the 80-foot walls of the Holy Place's inner sanctum, the dominating centerpiece of the Temple. He slowed to a walk as he entered the Holy Place. No matter how many times he had passed through the Holy Place, he had always felt a reverence, being in the center of Jewish worship.

Nicodemus stopped suddenly and observed the symbols of God's power: the huge golden seven-candled Menorah, the Table of Shewbread, and the veil. Then, in the corner of the Holy Place, segregated by two forty-foot curtains, was the Holy of Holies, which only one man could enter, the high priest.

Nicodemus always wondered about the Holy of Holies. If the Ark of the Covenant had not been seen by anyone except the high priest in over 400 years, was it still here in the Holy of Holies? Would the high priest admit that it was no longer there?

'Who could really say?' He realized he may never know the truth.

Nicodemus looked upward at the immense gilded Cherubs adorning the ceiling.

'Lord, you have my attention,' thought Nicodemus.

Nicodemus also knew the Temple represented the center of religious power of the Pharisees and Sadducees. Without a temple, how could they ever keep their Jewish traditions alive? How could they keep their covenants with God? And how would they keep their hold over the Jewish people? They would likely scatter to the four winds. Without the Temple, they were just wandering priests.

Nicodemus whispered a prayer. "Perhaps, Lord, if I am someday selected to be the high priest, I may see the Holy of Holies."

His communion was interrupted by Joseph.

"Take a left, past the Menorah, toward the brown curtain," barked Joseph.

Nicodemus complied, preoccupied by the continuous hammering echoing through the halls. The occasional wood plank dropped as apprentices and carpenters continued their efforts in the courtyards of the Temple.

Nicodemus looked around the Holy Place. The familiar sights so often brought to mind the inevitable question that had plagued his soul since he was committed to serve as a Levite priest when still a young boy.

'I have known no other life than serving my God by protecting and maintaining this Temple and the Torah. As my father,

and his fathers before him, since the time of Moses, we have been faithful to our God.'

'What would a normal life be like?' He imagined traveling to foreign lands, learning strange customs, and befriending the unbeliever. He had heard of exotic animals, forests that seem to go on forever, seas that never end, and beautiful women beyond imagination.

Shaking his head, Nicodemus reminded himself that the temptations of the world were a sin.

'I am a servant of God, chosen to be a spiritual leader. We have been conquered so many times. First in Egypt, then by Babylonians, Greeks, and now Romans. Someday we will find our freedom, but we need God's help. First, I must learn to obey, then I can lead.'

As they approached the corner of the western wall of the Holy Place, Joseph pointed to a plain brown embroidered curtain. "Pull back the curtain, just enough so we can pass."

Nicodemus followed Joseph's instructions but wondered why the Holy Place contained such a plain curtain in a corner of the inner sanctum. The curtain stood out like an unmarked rag crying for adornment, in contrast to the gold- and silver-embroidered tapestries, golden trays, and ornate furniture of the Priests' Court and Holy Place. It was as though someone had forgotten to replace the plain woolen cloth with a more ornate and appropriate drapery.

'It must be a temporary supply room for temple workers.'

Pulling back the heavy cloth, he saw that the entrance to the room was an uncharacteristically simple wooden door.

From the corner of his eye, Nicodemus watched as Joseph handed him a ring dangling with seven pitted and rusty keys.

"Unlock and open the door," Joseph ordered curtly.

After inserting six of the keys, he sighed. Of course, it was always the last key selected that worked. Fumbling with the only key without a symbol on its handle, he finally managed to unlock the heavy wooden door. Frustrated, Nicodemus pushed hard.

Taunting, the door remained stoically unmoved. Nicodemus used both arms and his left shoulder to force the door open enough to let both enter the pitch-black room.

Inhaling a nose full of disturbed dust, Nicodemus sneezed. "This room hasn't seen much use lately." Nicodemus looked around and found a stack of torches leaning against a wall behind the door. He retrieved three torches, lit one, and hung another in the holder on the wall near the door. After lighting a torch for Joseph, he looked around to inspect the room. A decade of dust covered the room, yet the stale air was still breathable despite the lack of any obvious ventilation.

Nicodemus then locked his eyes onto a four-foot gold menorah, decorated with symbols of the twelve tribes of the Hebrews. *'Why was this ceremonial menorah stored in this room?'* he questioned.

After a moment of hesitation, he lit the candles of the ancient menorah, bringing greater vision to the musty room.

Overwhelmed by the ambient dust in the air, Nicodemus sneezed several more times and looked around again. The room had transformed into a library, filled with stacks of ancient parchments and scrolls, all covered with dust that betrayed both their antiquity and neglect. Around him were four wooden tables, evidently used to record and read the parchments. Nicodemus slowly walked over to the nearest of the three-legged chairs, put his foot on the seat, and watched the decayed chair break into pieces, stirring up another dust cloud.

'Why hadn't this room been cleaned and organized like other libraries in the temple?' Nicodemus's curiosity overwhelmed him.

"What are these parchments?" he asked.

Irritated, Joseph shot back. "Never mind, they're just inventories." Joseph suddenly knelt and pulled a dirty rug from the floor. "Hand me that broom."

Nicodemus looked back at Joseph's dismissal with agitation. *'Wooden boxes, stuffed with ancient parchments and scrolls, he said this room was used for inventories. But why are the ornamental robes stacked on top of the tables? Again, Caiaphas is playing his political games with me. You can never get the whole truth from him . . . just shades of half-truths and distractions when you ask the wrong question.'*

'Why are we here?' Nicodemus knew better than to ask the obvious question and initiate another outburst. Reluctantly, he grimaced and simply complied with Joseph's instructions, handing him the straw broom leaning against the near wall. Well, at least the straw was still intact.

Joseph clutched the broom and pushed the dirt from a section of the floor. He then lifted a rug, pulling it to the corner of the room. Dust swirled as thin lines began to reveal the outline of a hatch.

Nicodemus stood behind Joseph as he pulled out his dagger and traced the lines of the hatch, and then reached back to take the keys from Nicodemus's belt. Nicodemus's curiosity was peaked. Joseph unlocked a latch in the floor and started to lift the floor hatch, which was large enough to allow someone to pass into the black abyss below.

Nicodemus knelt beside Joseph and both men lifted the heavy hatch, a gust of wind from underneath the floor whirled around them, instigating another flurry of dust. Their eyes flooded with tears as they blinked rapidly, desperately trying to clear the dust.

Nicodemus wiped his eyes and lowered his torch toward the lower room. He waited another moment for the dust to clear. Narrow, wooden, rough-hewn stairs became visible leading down into the dark.

"Light your torch and when you get into the chamber, light the torches hanging on the walls," commanded Joseph. He had the anxious and excited expression of a child about to open a present.

Nicodemus, on the other hand, had serious apprehensions, but knowing he had very little choice, moved into the black hole and balanced his right foot on the first step.

As he cautiously moved down the creaky stairs, all he could think about was the fragile chair he had crushed with the weight of his foot. He expected bats to fly up at him, chasing away any remaining courage he could muster. At last, he reached the bottom and Nicodemus saw the dim outline of a wooden door to his left. He looked around the first chamber, anticipating torture racks and skeletal remains. Relieved, he realized it was just an empty room.

"I'm coming down, make sure you're out of my way!" Joseph shouted as he gripped the single wooden railing of the stairs. "I fell when I came down here five years ago. Fortunately, all the stairs were replaced after that. Be careful though, rabbis are not carpenters!" Joseph chuckled. "Open the door with the key marked with the same symbol as the notch on the door."

Fumbling again with the keys, Nicodemus needed a full minute to examine each key while also balancing his torch. He finally found the key with the symbol for Abraham.

"Hurry up, we have another five doors after this one," snapped Joseph.

Nicodemus forced a key into the lock and turned. The door didn't budge.

"Kick it!" demanded Joseph.

He kicked the door, dislodging dirt from the hinges, and it sprang open.

"Light the torches on the walls as you pass them."

Nicodemus could only nod in compliance.

As they walked into the dark passageway, thoughts surfaced in his mind. '*Why did they choose me to become one of the Select?*' Nicodemus was one of the youngest priests to reach the role of Pharisee. When he was selected to the Sanhedrin council, he couldn't help but feel special, as though God Himself had chosen him for something extraordinary. Three years later, when Joseph Caiaphas approached him about the Council of the Select, he was stunned by the invitation.

Nicodemus had heard rumors that there were smaller leadership councils within the Great Sanhedrin, and these rumors were validated when Joseph informed him of an opportunity to fill a vacancy in the Select. Initially, Nicodemus hesitated to accept the honor, knowing how Joseph was well-known for his ambitions within the Pharisees. He wasn't sure he could trust Joseph's political maneuvers.

In the end, Nicodemus decided that he couldn't pass up the opportunity, even if it was burdened with risk. For the past six months, Nicodemus had been tested by the remaining six members. It was only yesterday he learned that he'd been accepted and took the vows of secrecy that required him to dedicate his life to the Council of the Select. Today, it seemed that Joseph would unveil the secret as to why the Select existed.

Suddenly, Joseph started shouting, startling Nicodemus. "Move, Nicodemus. The torches won't burn forever."

Past the first door, Nicodemus found another hatch at the end of the tunnel, this time with a lock.

"Open the hatch. The symbol will be on the key."

Once again, Nicodemus rummaged for the matching key to the symbol for "time" on the hatch. Both men lifted the wooden barrier to unveil another set of stairs.

Nicodemus lit a torch from the wall and threw it down the wooden stairs onto the floor below, scattering a dozen rats across the room. He stepped onto the stairs and entered the next chamber.

"Hurry. We have three more chambers to descend before we reach our destination."

Nicodemus looked around and saw another locked floor hatch, this one with the symbol of a shepherd's staff. Accessing the next three chambers went quickly as Nicodemus adapted to the rhythm of unlocking the doors and hatches, throwing torches down the stairs to scatter the rats, then quickly identifying the matching symbol and key. After thirty minutes, they arrived in an open hallway.

"Light the torches on the right and I'll light those on the left. When you get to the end of the hall, it will branch out into two circular elevated walkways. Continue lighting the torches until we meet at the opposite side of the hall. But be careful! There is no railing, and the chamber floor is ten feet below."

Again, Nicodemus followed Joseph's orders, lighting the torches in the hall and then turning right. Below, he could only see darkness. After skimming the circular ledge of the chamber and lighting several torches, shadows became visible below.

"What are we looking for?" he shouted.

"Quiet! You'll see soon enough."

Once the torches were lit on the circular ledge above the chamber, Nicodemus could make out that the chamber below was filled with shelves of scrolls and ornate containers in twelve concentric circles. In the center was a large particularly ornate container, seemingly made of gold.

Nicodemus turned to Joseph, gasping, "What am I looking at?"

Joseph pointed to a wide set of stone stairs leading down into the chamber. He started to descend, lighting more torches along the way.

"You are looking at the history and wealth of the twelve tribes of the Hebrews, Nicodemus. And God's covenant."

Nicodemus stood above him on the ledge in amazement. The torches' circle of light began to reveal more and more ancient scrolls, archives, golden chests, and golden menorahs. Nicodemus felt frozen in place. He tried to move but could not. He gazed, transfixed, at the item in the very center of the treasures—a large crate covered by a large ornate tapestry. Over time, one corner of the tapestry had torn, exposing the tip of a large golden wing.

Joseph's approach to the middle of the chamber woke Nicodemus up from his astonishment. He took a deep breath, pointed, and asked in a voice full of awe, "Is that the, the, the . . . ?"

CONFINING WALLS

Tribune Silus Valens missed the open spaces of Italy, his homeland. Especially his farm, north of Rome, which provided frequent opportunities for him to get away from his official responsibilities. In Jerusalem, he found it difficult to find a sense of privacy, and he often felt trapped inside the city. Due to the frequent Zealot raids, venturing outside the city had become risky, if not outright dangerous. Even riding in the country required several guards to ensure his safety.

A few years ago, Silus found a partial antidote to feeling trapped. Before dawn, he would run up the stairs of the fortress walls in full battle gear, then continue around the walls and towers of Fortress Antonia. It was his way of seeing the whole fortress and also staying in fighting shape. Besides keeping him in good physical condition, the routine gave him a unique and informative perspective of his fortress and Jerusalem.

Each morning, Silus looked westward upon the city of Jerusalem and south over the Hebrew Temple. What surprised Silus about the city was the similarity of activities in the adjoining Temple and the fortress itself. He observed the immutable routines of people—women, children, servants, and soldiers, all gathering water from the outlets of the Gihon Springs. Shortly after, the same women and support troops started preparing breakfast meals. Like a choreographed concert following the same music script, the rising pitch of human activity within the fortress, inside the Temple, and below in the city of Jerusalem became a symphony of human activity that signaled the new day, like the Greek sirens of Anthemoessa.

This morning, Silus paused in his circuit to think about his new training plan for the Xth Legion. Overlooking the Temple, Silus noted a different activity than what he had been accustomed to seeing. Standing atop the southeast tower that overlooked the Temple he saw two Pharisees, running up the rampart into the Temple. In this early morning hour, they seemed unusually hurried, rushing with purpose. Silus' curiosity was aroused. It was not a festival or holiday today. No special events were expected. Why was the Temple choir also on the steps, preparing their songs, hours before their normal routine? Silus was trained to spot a diversion, and this was an obvious diversion by the Pharisees. Odd.

Chapter 2

A TIME TO FIGHT

16 AD
FORTRESS ANTONIA, JERUSALEM

Cassius heard the gasp of air he had just inhaled, trying to fill his lungs in one desperate attempt to breathe. The wheezing of his parched throat announced to everyone his struggle.

'Air . . . more air!' Shaking his head to clear the sweat from his face, he involuntarily closed his eyes from the sting of the salty sweat that poured into his eyes.

Two hours past sunrise and already the fortress courtyard air was stagnant, as heat radiated off the 60-foot white stone walls. Making matters worse, these same walls prevented any cooling from a morning Mediterranean breeze.

'I'm parched,' Cassius mouthed, trying to find enough moisture to wet his tongue. He realized the heat was draining his reserves, he was reaching his physical limits.

'I won't yield!' he grimaced; his facial muscles hardened as he demanded that his body fight despite the pain.

Cassius could not stop the sweat from burning his eyes, all he could see was a blur of his opponent. His knuckles turned white as he held his sword even tighter, ensuring his soaked palms maintained a grip on the only weapon he had to survive that morning. As his sword struck Bracus's shield, Cassius watched his sweat splatter across his attacker's chest. For another five minutes, he pounded his sword against Bracus's shield again and again with little effect other than shooting pain up his arm.

He looked down and his hands were shaking. *'My fingers are starting to cramp, they're numb. I have to move now, or he'll take me down!'* thought Cassius.

In the possible chance of ending this struggle, Cassius tightened his grip and hammered his sword even harder. Aiming his swing lower, he finally struck the flesh on Bracus's upper thigh.

Cassius watched as his opponent's muscled legs rippled and twitched, absorbing the blow. Yet he knew that Bracus would not yield. Instinctively, Cassius twisted his shoulders to the right, raising the wooden sword to strike again, prepared for the inevitable counterstrike.

As he raised his arm, Cassius saw a gathering shadow from the corners of his eyes. Men were running towards them. Soon a crowd began to surround the two men fighting in the courtyard. He could hear yelling from a distance, unsure what the words meant. It was just noise, a distraction.

Cassius pushed his mind and body to continue fighting, forcing himself to ignore his own desperate need for more air, his muscle fatigue, and his pain.

Sweat continued to cascade down his forehead, collecting dust as it traveled into swollen eyes and then overflowing and running down his cheeks. Cassius had nothing to clear his face other that his bare forearm.

'I need time to breathe. Have to push him back . . .' Shaking his head wildly, half blind from sweat, Cassius swung his sword in broad sweeps toward Bracus's midsection.

Cassius then realized his last wild blow was a signal, he was starting to lose the tactical advantage. He turned quickly, barely avoiding a glancing blow to his shoulder.

Looking up into Bracus's desperate eyes, Cassius realized Bracus was also at the limit of human endurance. *'He'll make a desperate counterattack.'*

Cassius then saw Bracus mouthing garbled words, breathing heavily between gasps of air and thrusts of his wooden sword. Moments later Cassius finally processed Bracus's words. "Your loincloth has fallen off!"

Cassius looked down. "Damn!" he yelled, angered by his own reflex to stop and look, even though he knew it was a ruse. Fighting the resistance of his own failing body, Cassius commanded his muscles to move one more time.

But Bracus had already moved low, using his leverage to shove Cassius in the abdomen, forcing him backward. Cassius grunted as he staggered off balance, extending his right leg and arm to pivot on the gravel, preventing himself from falling. Rolling to his right, he staggered upward again, five yards from Bracus.

'Move your arms!' Cassius demanded his right arm to move. *'Swing again at Bracus.'*

This time his longer arms carried the wooden sword across Bracus's lower ribcage. Bracus turned in pain and continued his swing, rounding his sword in a full-circle attack toward Cassius's right.

Cassius knew he could count on Bracus's temper to swing wildly. He used the last of his strength for a desperate counter move and then the wooden swords met at the center of the arc between the two men.

Cassius watched in slow motion as wooden swords chipped with the first encounter, and then shattered on the second blow.

Both men stood wavering back and forth, intense eyes staring at each other waiting for the other to make the next move. Sucking in gulps of air, they nodded to each other, relaxed, and dropped the broken hilts of their swords, falling to their knees. Cassius bowed his head, saturated with sweat, and covered with mud from the courtyard gravel. He raised his head again to see Bracus trying to lift himself to stand, eyes glazed and swollen red with sweat.

'He's getting harder to beat,' Cassius realized.

Too exhausted to talk, he just looked at the man who had grown up as his best friend. Bracus caught his eyes and smiled. Then Bracus heaved his breakfast onto the courtyard, wobbled, and fell over backward in his feeble attempt to stand, laughing as he fell.

As the two friends lay prostrate in the courtyard sand, their eyes refocused on the shadows that had surrounded them during the fight. The Roman garrison stood in a circle around Cassius and Bracus, just a few yards from the exhausted fighters. Soldiers were laughing and shouting at the top of their lungs, exhilarated by the exhibition they had just witnessed.

"I told you Cassius would best him!" came a shout from inside the ring of soldiers.

Another round of laughter and shouting was quickly silenced by the approaching officer, Centurion Orestes.

Orestes stood over Cassius and Bracus as they lay on the courtyard gravel, his eyes wide in amazement. He shook his head and started to laugh. "Your loincloth has fallen? Bracus, I'll have to remember that when we fight Zealots."

Exhausted and unable to laugh, Bracus just smiled. "It worked, sir."

"You'd better clean up and get some lunch. You have guard duty in four hours at Prefect Ambivulus' palace." Centurion Orestes laughed at his two young soldiers and then shook his head in wonder. '*Where did this intensity come from?*' he wondered.

"The rest of you, get back to your drills!" ordered Centurion Orestes. As he did, he glanced up at the corner of the eastern fortress wall and saw a lone figure watching the spectacle from above. He realized there would be questions he could not answer about the exercise fight between Cassius and Bracus. Orestes looked back at the prostrate soldiers trying to recover from their exhaustion.

Laying in the gravel courtyard, Cassius was leaning on his left elbow, holding his right hand as his face contorted with obvious signs of agony.

After gripping his sword during the fight with all his remaining strength, Cassius's right hand finally lost the struggle against cramping. Pulsating quivers of razor-edged pain shot through his fingers like lightning bolts as they contorted in unnatural positions. Cassius grimaced as he gently massaged his paralyzed fingers with his left hand, forcing them to work again.

Swearing as he stammered, attempting to stand up, he shouted. "If you weren't so stubborn, Bracus!"

Leaning over to Bracus, Cassius extended his left hand and had to lean backward with all his remaining strength to pull Bracus upright. Bracus cringed and grumbled as Cassius grabbed his waist belt for leverage.

As they walked away, Cassius quietly admitted. "Dad would have been proud of us today, Bracus. I am so glad you're here. I wouldn't have joined the army without you." Bracus smiled and wrapped his left arm around Cassius's shoulders. Together they hobbled back to the barracks.

Looking around he marveled at the construction of the fortress. He felt safe inside the Roman fortress, inside the solid 60-foot granite walls. Turning to Bracus, he pondered aloud.

"We have been brought to such a strange land, Bracus."

Bracus looked over with a blank look on his face. "Cassius, when I become a tribune, I'll explain the world to you. But now, I just want a bath."

OLD SOLDIERS

Standing on the southern fortress walls 60 feet above the courtyard, Tribune Silus Valens watched Centurion Orestes shake his head as he walked across the courtyard below. The Tribune nodded approval of the morning's weapons drills, then smiled.

Centurion Clavius Orestes walked across the courtyard, then looked up and stopped when he noticed Tribune Valens watching him from above, atop the fortress walls. Raising his hand to his chest, Clavius saluted and then saw Silus smile and shake his head. Clavius relaxed and returned his nod, trying to hide his own smile.

In the ten years that both Centurion Orestes and Tribune Valens had been stationed with the Roman Xth Legion in Jerusalem, they had never witnessed such intensity in the daily training exercises. For years, both had talked about ways to improve daily weapons drills to a level that replicated actual battle. But their desire to get their soldiers to train with the intensity that they fight, so future battles would not be so frightening, always seemed to fall short of expectations.

Today they witnessed two young soldiers demonstrate their aspirations for the Xth Legion. They trained like they were actually fighting!

It was perfectly clear to Tribune Valens that aggressive, realistic training was possible. No longer could the same mundane exercises be tolerated in the fortress. The young soldiers had set a new level of weapons training, from routine exercises to imitating actual fighting. Both Tribune Valens and Centurion Orestes knew the challenge they faced . . . to instill the same passion in their soldiers.

Valens thought to himself as he headed back to his living quarters. *'If I can get them to compete for a prize . . . extra time off or money. Would they train harder for rewards?'*

Valens knew a higher standard of training would save the lives of Legion soldiers in actual battle. His sandals clapped on the stone cobbled walkway atop the fortress walls as he hurried to his quarters. He needed to develop and write down his new training plan.

Turning a corner inside the fortress, Silus took off his helmet, ran his hand through his short black hair, and sighed. "I'm not sure I understand what I saw today, but I can't let this opportunity escape," he murmured.

Turning into a stairwell, Silus hurried down two flights of stairs, entered another long granite hallway, and turned left toward his apartment overlooking the fortress. The wooden door was already open.

At the doorway, Silus hesitated, raised his eyebrows, and instinctively put his right hand on his gladius sword. A lone figure stood looking out the south window. Cutting a slice of apple, the solitary man gazed out across the fortress, looking at the massive Jewish Temple.

Valens relaxed when he recognized the stocky five-foot-seven-inch silhouette of his longtime friend, and the highest-ranking Roman official in Judea and Samaria, Prefect Marcus Ambivulus.

"Can I offer you some wine, sir?" Silus smiled and started pouring the wine into brass cups, already knowing the answer.

"No need, I've already poured my own. Silus, sit down. We need to talk." Cutting another slice of apple, the prefect looked up at Silus. "Quite an exhibition this morning. I understand that the tall soldier today was Quintus Dias's son. The shorter soldier, Bracus, is his lifelong friend. Of course, I'd expect nothing less from the son of such a decorated soldier."

The prefect continued. "Is it true both grew up and were trained by Quintus?"

Silus returned with a cup of wine for himself. "Yes, I've already made inquiries as to the extent of their training."

Looking at his prefect, Silus sat quietly for a moment. Wrinkles surrounded his eyebrows as sadness combed over his face. "And yes, Marcus, it is true. Quintus was the best and bravest Legion officer I've ever known. Now his son is here with us."

Marcus laughed. "I remember Quintus Dias pulling you out of that hellhole in Germania twenty years ago, Silus. Those heathens were ready to roast you alive. You lived through that hell only because the two of you were the best centurions in all the Roman Legions."

"I haven't forgotten my debt to Quintus. I can't repay him in this blasted desert, but we can look out for his boys. I still can't understand why he married that Greek slave and bought that farm. She's a Hebrew, I think."

"There are days when I miss his friendship, too," admitted Marcus. "But more importantly, his honesty and loyalty. That's why I won't let you go too far from me, Silus. If I still had the two of you, I could march into Rome instead of fighting these renegade Zealots!"

Silus sat back, rubbed his unshaven face, and drank his wine. "What are we going to do with his boys? You are right, they were raised as brothers. I had gotten a letter from Quintus to watch over them when they arrived. They're too good for simple guard duty."

Marcus looked up at Silus, whose face betrayed his concerns for Quintus' boys. Yet Marcus ignored Silus's hesitations. "I know, Silus. That's why I wanted to talk. Accelerate their training. Test them. We've seen how they can fight, but can they think? If they are anything like Quintus, we'll need their skills. And their loyalty."

"And one more thing, Silus. Write a letter back to Quintus. Let him know we are watching over Cassius and Bracus. Tell him we'll bring the boys home when we return to Rome. Soon I hope."

Silus walked to the window overlooking the fortress. Soldiers filled the courtyard, still practicing weapons drills in their loincloths. Silus looked at his men with a grimace. Compared to the dramatic fighting between Cassius and Bracus earlier, his men looked like they were practicing in slow motion, trying to memorize the daily drills.

This can't be real. How did we accept that such lifeless motion was supposed to simulate fighting.' Silus frowned as he turned toward Marcus Ambivulus. Then Silus paused, hesitating before he addressed his prefect again.

"We owe Quintus so much, Marcus. His boys are young, we can't risk them unnecessarily in this forsaken land."

"And you are aware, Marcus, there is danger in this land. The Hebrews are a stubborn people. Even though they are vastly outnumbered, Jewish Zealots still have the audacity to attack our patrols. They never learn. They claim this land as theirs, despite being conquered so many times . . . Assyrians, Babylonians, Persians, Greeks. And now we are their masters. We conquered the Jews, but do we truly own this dry land?"

"And the people keep talking about a Messiah, a Hebrew king that will save them. If this future prophet gives them hope, the Jews will be harder to deal with. Damn these Hebrews, they are a persistent and hardheaded people. Either way, one day we'll have to crush their hope if we want to survive in this land."

"One more thing, Marcus, something is going on with the Pharisees. I saw two Pharisees enter the Temple very early this morning, running up the steps and getting the choir to start early as a diversion. They're up to something. Probably involving their hidden treasures."

"I know, Silus." Prefect Ambivulus stood up and started to walk out but stopped in the doorway. "Odd you would mention the Jew's treasure. I just received a letter from the Senate reminding us of our specific instructions."

"And?" asked Silus, raising his eyebrows and standing to meet Marcus' gaze.

"Our orders are to allow the Hebrews their religious freedoms, if they are under control. But don't let down our guard. Do not allow them to believe they can gain freedom. Use whatever measures deemed necessary, Silus. Blame the Zealots and the Pharisees for their misfortunes. Fortress Antonia is here for that reason, and to make sure the Jews' treasures eventually go back to Rome. If the symbol of their God's covenant becomes known, it could lead to widespread religious revolt. The Sanhedrin are wise to keep it hidden."

Marcus paused and let out a sigh of sadness. "And aside from all that, I'm homesick too, Silus. We both are. It's been too long."

GUARD DUTY

Cassius let out a sigh and looked over to Bracus as he pulled his chest plate over his tunic. *I'll be sore tomorrow morning.*

Bracus is getting stronger, faster. I was close to getting my butt kicked today.'

Across the barebones barracks, Bracus was frowning, trying to untangle his bronze chest plate from his tunic. "It's always the same," Bracus said. "Checking merchants for weapons and saluting officers. Can we at least try to save someone or stop assassins for a change?" He pulled his shirt from underneath his breastplate.

Cassius laughed as he visualized his next comment. "Well, if you prefer, I can get you a dress so you can pretend you're a young lady in distress."

Cassius smiled as he walked between the rows of wooden bunks to the weapons locker to gather their swords and lances.

"I'd just like a few hours to relax and a quiet day standing guard at the entrance of the prefect's palace. My muscles need the rest," he murmured, out of hearing from Bracus who was still struggling to get his chest plate over his tunic.

Suddenly an object flew past Cassius's head and hit the wall. Looking around, Cassius identified the remains of a ripe pomegranate lying on the ground.

Cassius turned and quipped at Bracus. "Okay. Perhaps I'll play the part of an old woman. Even though you'd fit the part much better."

Laughing, Cassius started to run but quickly felt a solid pomegranate strike the back of his left shoulder.

It was four hours of standing, saluting, and then leaning against the entrance of Prefect Ambivulus's palace, when no one was around, that led to the need to pass the time. Cassius started to quiz Bracus on their understanding of Greek while Bracus retaliated with questions on Greek and Roman history. After hours of questions and arguing about the right answers, their heads hurt as well as their bodies. Just as their watch was about to end, they saw Prefect Ambivulus walking back to his home, followed by an entourage of junior officers. Cassius quickly stood at attention as he recognized the prefect. Bracus, leaning against the polished marble walls of the palace, snapped to attention immediately after Cassius.

Approaching his palace, Prefect Ambivulus stopped and looked directly at his two young guards. "Your loin cloth has fallen." He murmured as he passed the two young men. His entourage of junior officers laughed as they passed Cassius and Bracus.

Cassius kept his gaze forward as they saluted their prefect and junior officers. Once they had passed, Cassius looked over to Bracus in surprise.

"Even the prefect knows about today's fight!" Cassius scowled at Bracus. "Now everyone in the Legion will be giving us grief for that comment!"

Fifteen minutes later, Cassius was still frustrated but managed a smile when he looked up to see their reliefs. He welcomed the sight of the two guards approaching them.

"At last! We can have the afternoon free," Bracus shouted.

As the guards approached, Cassius overheard both soldiers arguing about the 10 drachmae they had won wagering on today's impromptu 'fight' between Cassius and Bracus.

"I told you we should have wagered more on Cassius," one responded.

Cassius smiled at Bracus and shrugged his shoulders. Bracus just glared back at Cassius. "I won the fight you know!" Bracus declared.

Cassius just winked at Bracus, knowing it would bother him for the rest of the day.

Finally relieved from guard duties, the two friends, tired and sore, began walking back to the barracks.

Two blocks from the palace, Cassius hesitated, smiled, and turned toward Bracus. "I have a surprise for you. I talked to the sergeant at the stables yesterday. He's been complaining about having too many garrison horses to exercise, so I volunteered to help if you are interested." Pausing with a smirk, Cassius continued, "Though I'd understand if you're too tired from 'winning' the drills today."

"What? We have horses to ride?" Bracus's mood immediately brightened at the news. "Why are we going back to the fortress? Let's head to the stables. The ride will help relax our muscles from the beating I gave you this morning."

Cassius raised his arms to stretch the shoulder muscles, readjusted his breastplate, and chuckled. "We'll need our armor on if we ride in the city. Let's go."

As Cassius walked into the fortress stables, he looked around and inhaled the aroma of hay, grain, and horses. His thoughts drifted back to his boyhood farm in Tuscany. '*Home . . . this reminds me of home. The smell of wheat in the barn after the fall harvest. Brushing down our horses, cleaning stalls.*' Cassius's face twinged as he felt the soft pangs of homesickness.

A half-hour later, Cassius mounted a young horse, still frisky from being left to stand in the stalls for two weeks. Reaching down, he stroked the neck of his young gelding, letting his legs fall to wrap around the chest of his horse. He slipped his sandals into the stirrups and the gelding bolted forward. Cassius laughed as his grey horse cantered sideways, pleading to run.

The sergeant laughed as he watched Bracus and Cassius jockey outside the paddock, both horses twisting and jumping with excitement from the newfound riders and a chance to run. "If you break your heads, I won't be at fault!" the sergeant warned as they rode the geldings toward the fortress gates.

Bracus grinned with joy. For once they were going to ride spirited horses instead of the older tired horses they had been given. It wasn't long before their equine companions began to test their riding skills. Cassius pulled his gelding's head around as the horse spun in circles. Bracus was also struggling to control his gelding, unabashedly cursing as he laughed.

After the third attempt to free themselves from their riders, Cassius gave his horse a swift kick in the ribs, turning his gelding's head in circles until the horse finally gave up his impressive attempts and yielded control. Still laughing, Bracus followed Cassius's example and established dominance over his horse.

"Bracus . . . We'll never be able to ride them through Jerusalem if we can't get control of these horses," Cassius stated.

Holding his reins tight and guiding the horse with his legs, Cassius looked over to Bracus and nodded that it was time to move the horses forward. The pair negotiated the market awkwardly at first, toppling over two merchant carts which further spooked the young spirited horses.

But as they trotted away, Cassius couldn't help but look back at the Jewish merchants. Cassius's face cringed as a wave of guilt cascaded over his mind. Merchants were scrambling to pick up apples, pomegranates, and bags of grain from the fallen carts. They were swearing at the recklessness of the Roman horsemen.

Cassius looked around and felt the anger of their hearts. He knew the merchants could only see two arrogant Roman soldiers riding through their marketplace. He realized they could not see his embarrassment. They could not know that Cassius and Bracus were also once farmers and understood the hard work of gathering crops and trying to sell their produce in the market.

Cassius and Bracus were just trying to corral the young horses into obedience. Regardless of the circumstances, Cassius could hear his father's words. *"You are responsible for the horse you ride, son. You are the rider in command of the horse, the horse doesn't control you!"*

He turned his horse to yell his apologies. '*I have no money to compensate these men,*' he swore to himself. Suddenly his horse spun around in a circle. Cassius kicked the gelding in the ribs to free themselves from causing any further harm to the merchants and their customers. Cassius sighed, feeling stupid for allowing himself to ride into the crowded market.

'*I have to make amends . . .*' he promised. "Bracus, we'll need to come back and find these farmers . . . we need to pay for damages!" Bracus nodded in agreement, knowing he could not argue with Cassius about his sense of responsibility. Too busy controlling his own gelding, Bracus spurred his horse forward.

Finally passing the crowded market into open streets, the young horses began to calm in the wider streets of Jerusalem. Trotting over the cobbled stones, the geldings heads and tails were fully erect, full of excitement for the possibility of open spaces and a chance to gallop. After several blocks of controlled riding, Cassius came to a corner and stopped. He turned to Bracus, annoyed, squinting to focus his eyes at the next street intersection. "Ahead, at the next street—look!"

Bracus stopped his horse short, twisting the dark bay gelding's head around, and turned toward Cassius's gaze. At the intersection of the next market, a Roman officer was mounted on a black stallion.

"He's waving for us to come over," Cassius quietly told Bracus. His face betrayed his frustration, frowning as he understood their afternoon's freedom was at risk.

"So much for our afternoon ride!" Bracus said aloud.

'We could turn and pretend we didn't see the officer,' thought Cassius. He was hesitant to give up their afternoon of freedom. Knowing better, he overcame his initial desire to ride away. Cassius slowly led the pair toward the Roman officer.

"Quiet. Follow my lead," Cassius responded to Bracus. "Perhaps the afternoon is not all lost."

As they approached, Cassius suddenly had a clear view of the horse the officer was riding. In front of him stood a muscled, immaculately groomed black Andalusian. Cassius had never seen a stallion like this before. His jaw dropped and his eyebrows raised as he stared at the horse.

Suddenly self-aware of his gapping stare, he closed his mouth and cleared his throat. The Andalusian in turn raised his head and tail, his thick black mane bouncing in the air as he shook the flies from his face. As the sun beamed off the horse's contoured muscles, the Andalusian stood poised as though he were a statute.

The Roman officer coughed, amused that Cassius had been mesmerized by his horse. Cassius and Bracus simultaneously looked up and immediately recognized Prefect Ambivulus, disguised in a plain officer's uniform. Halting their horses, the pair saluted, hands slapping their chests and extending their arms in tribute.

"Perfect Ambivulus!"

"Well, it seems that I am honored to have such distinguished guards again today. Tell me your names, soldiers." But Marcus Ambivulus stared at Cassius as though he already knew him.

Cassius replied, "Sir, I am Cassius Dias, and this is Bracus Antivius."

Cassius twisted in his saddle, uneasy with the highest-ranking Roman officer in Judea asking him questions.

'Taking orders is easy when there's only one reply: Yes, sir,' thought Cassius.

But then, Cassius knew his anxieties escaped his control anytime he had a conversation with a superior officer, especially his centurion. So, he did what was safe—he kept his mouth shut whenever possible.

Marcus watched the two young soldiers and recognized their unease. He raised his eyebrows as he watched Cassius's obvious discomfort. Marcus Ambivulus looked around and decided to break the tension with his young guards. He smiled and then nodded to the boys: "Follow me. I need to exercise my horse outside the walls of Jerusalem. You'll have the pleasure of escorting me today, as well as guarding my home."

In one movement, Marcus Ambivulus turned his stallion, and without a hint of enticement, allowed his young

Andalusian to launch into a canter toward the east gate. Startled, Cassius hesitated then squeezed his horse with his calves, pushing his gelding into the pursuit of Prefect Ambivulus. Cassius looked back, relieved to see Bracus just off his right flank.

As soon as Marcus Ambivulus cleared the gate and pedestrian traffic, he also looked back to ensure his guards were following. He then leaned forward, the signal that gave his stallion permission to accelerate into a full gallop.

Surprised, Cassius yelled at Bracus, "Follow him!" They squeezed their horses into a full gallop to catch up.

Marcus and his stallion continued to move farther ahead, despite Cassius's best efforts to push his horse faster. Cassius was desperate not to lose his Prefect Ambivulus. *'How could I explain that to Centurion Orestes?'* Gripping with his legs, he leaned forward and kicked the sides of his horse with his heels, pushing his horse for more speed.

"Faster, we need to run faster," Cassius begged his gelding. Looking back again, Cassius grinned as he saw his best friend engulfed in a cloud of dust.

"Bracus, faster!" he shouted. "There will be hell to pay if we lose the prefect!"

Wiping the dust from his eyes and face with his tunic, Bracus leaned forward and spurred his horse to run faster.

Cassius followed the road around a bend leading east, looking for the dust of Prefect Ambivulus's horse. Around the corner, Cassius found Marcus Ambivulus still galloping 100 yards ahead. They galloped their horses for another two miles then turned right off the road following their prefect onto a small path leading south toward several hills. After another half mile, they finally started to slow the horses at the edge of an olive and pine grove nestled at the base of a small hill. The prefect turned, slowed his stallion, and looked back at his two new guardians, still behind him and still pushing their horses to catch up.

'*So, they are good riders as well.*' Ambivulus thought as he dismounted and walked the Andalusian to cool down the horse. Sweat drenched the black stallion, accentuating the contours of his well-developed muscles. Despite the four-mile gallop, the prefect's Andalusian held its head aloft, eyes on the geldings, acknowledging the lesser horses.

As Cassius and Bracus approached, they slowed their horses to a controlled canter, then to a trot to begin the process of cooling the horses.

Cassius instinctively looked around. They were surrounded by a small forest of trees with a freshwater brook on the right of the surrounding hills. He took in the scent of the Aleppo pines, and the cooling breeze passing through the trees. The silver-green olive trees provided excellent shade for the horses and riders in the heat of the late August afternoon. But the trees also provided good cover for anyone who wanted to surprise the prefect and his guards. '*I feel uneasy about this place.*' Cassius leaned toward Bracus. "We need to keep sharp eyes here, we're off the main road and too isolated outside of the fortress and Jerusalem's walls."

They both turned as they heard the prefect's voice. "Wait until your horses cool before you give them water."

Cassius raised his brow; he felt this order was unnecessary. "Yes, sir," he responded. In truth, he welcomed his prefect's concern for the horses. His order told Cassius more about this officer than most would realize.

Marcus Ambivulus smiled at Cassius and Bracus with approval. They had already removed their saddles and blankets and were walking their geldings in the shade of the trees, refusing to allow them to eat the grass until they had cooled.

Marcus Ambivulus walked toward Cassius and Bracus. "You have ridden well today. And I see you know how to care for your horses. Cassius, did you learn this from your father?"

Cassius looked up and saluted the prefect, awkwardly searching for the appropriate answer. "Yes, sir, my father taught us both to ride, and not to abuse our horses."

"What else did he teach you in Tuscany?"

Cassius hesitated. He had never disclosed where they had grown up.

Realizing his revealing statement, Prefect Ambivulus continued. "Yes, Cassius, I knew your father. He served with me in defeating the Gauls in Germania. He's a good man, an excellent soldier of Rome. But now I understand he's a farmer. You remind me of him."

The prefect continued, "Did Quintus tell you about his adventures in the Ist Roman Legion?"

"No, sir. He never talked about being a Roman soldier. But he did teach us how to use the sword, to hunt with the bow. My father did his best to teach us how to survive."

"First, Quintus Dias wasn't just a plain soldier. He was the Senior Centurion of the Ist Roman Legion in Germania," responded Prefect Ambivulus. Looking at Cassius, he could tell he was dumbstruck to learn his father was a senior centurion.

"Let me tell you a true story about your father."

6 BC

1ST ROMAN LEGION IN GERMANIA

"It was snowing during that winter night, twenty-two years ago. After pushing 4,000 Gauls eastward for two weeks, we were camped in a clearing surrounded by pine trees just west of the Rhine River.

"The Gauls were hard fighters, passionate. And deadly. It was their land, they understood how to fight in the forests. And they knew they could never face us in open land, where we could organize. And we had the advantage of cavalry. That's why a meadow in the woods seemed perfect, we could organize and use our cavalry. At least that's what we believed.

"That night, your dad, Centurion Quintus Dias, was riding through the encampment, checking each tent to ensure his soldiers had a fire and enough wood to burn through the night. A north wind was blowing; it was bitter cold.

"Your dad's best friend was Silus Valens, a newly promoted Centurion who was checking the sentries, ensuring they were awake and instructing them to keep moving to avoid frostbite. It's odd, but both your dad and Silus could feel a fight coming. Somehow, they suspected there was danger in the woods . . . the pitch-black meadow was also perfect for an ambush.

"By 2 o'clock in the morning, the snow had stopped, and an eerie silence permeated the air. Normally, you would hear owls or blackbirds mocking us through the night. But there was nothing but dead silence. Even the wind abandoned us that night.

"Then all hell broke loose. From the surrounding woods came the Gauls, thousands of them . . . yelling and shooting flaming arrows. They were running so fast that our soldiers only had moments to get out of their tents and try to arm themselves. They had even painted themselves blue and looked like ghosts in the firelight.

"The initial wave of Gauls was devastating. The Ist Legion lost hundreds of men in the first few minutes that night. Half asleep and disoriented, they couldn't rally to a defensive ring, most didn't even have their shields.

"Silus Valens and his men were closest to the attack of the Gauls. Silus's century of men were quickly surrounded, the first line of soldiers were killed by flaming arrows and screaming ghosts coming out of the woods. To make it worse, Gauls had made fire wagons and were pushing them into Silus's formation of soldiers. By some miracle, Silus was able to get the soldiers he had left into a defensive circle, but the Gauls were starting to overwhelm them. Despite the snow, fires were burning everywhere.

"I was watching from a high point on the other side of the camp when I saw your dad turning his horse straight towards the Gaul's attack that surrounded Silus and his soldiers. Quintus was leading his 600 soldiers directly into the mass of heathens to save Valens and his men. Then, without waiting for his soldiers, Quintus galloped directly into the middle of the savages, beating a wedge through the Gauls so his men could follow. Quintus fought like a madman to save his best friend, fighting with a frenzy that I'll never forget. It was the bravest act I've ever seen.

"Quintus and his men finally fought their way into the middle of Silus' broken formation of soldiers, where they joined forces and turned on the Gauls. Within minutes they began pushing back the attack. By the time the sun rose that morning, a thousand wounded and dead bodies were scattered across the meadow . . . The remaining Gauls were gone, driven back into the woods. Your father saved us that night. Silus owes him his life. We all do. "

THE OLIVE GROVE ATTACK

Cassius and Bracus stood watching Prefect Ambivulus, unable to utter a word, trying to absorb the magnitude of the story about Cassius's father. Both boys only knew Cassius's father as a farmer and family man. They only knew his big hands for cradling newborn lambs or driving ox plows to harrow corn and wheat fields. They could not imagine Cassius's father as a legendary hero in the Roman Ist Legion.

Cassius and Bracus paused and looked quietly at each other. They were amazed and now homesick.

Prefect Ambivulus broke the silence with a question. "And your mother. I heard she was a Greek tutor for the Roman Senators before your father bought her freedom. What did you learn from her?"

The prefect's question shook Cassius back into the present. Cassius hesitated again, taken aback by his Prefect Ambivulus's knowledge of his family.

"My mother taught us to read, write, do mathematics, and understand Greek and Aramaic." But before Cassius could answer further, the sound of crushing dried leaves interrupted him.

Cassius looked up and saw two armed Zealots coming down the hill from the east, running between the olive and pine trees. They held their spears high in the air, ready to throw, as they maneuvered between the trees.

Marcus Ambivulus saw the approaching threat as well but was reassured when his two guardians drew their swords and turned to form a protective semicircle around him. But he also knew just two Zealots would not attack three armed Roman soldiers. There must have been more rebels in the woods.

No one moved as the three men watched the approaching Zealots. Seconds later, an arrow whistled past Cassius and lodged in the bare ground, coming from another direction. With a thud, another arrow struck a tree branch three feet away from the prefect's chest.

"Horses!" Cassius shouted to Bracus, realizing the horses were their only means of quick escape and needed to be safely away from the ensuing fight. Bracus ran to take the reins of the startled geldings. He carefully but quickly approached the Andalusian, who thankfully, allowed his reins to be taken. Bracus led the three horses away from the inevitable fight to a cluster of olive trees on the opposite side of the brook where he deftly tied the reins to a solid-looking branch and hurried back to join his best friend in the inevitable conflict.

Cassius, having taken a defensive position to protect his superior instinctively knew one key fact. In battle, seconds matter.

Turning to confirm where the prefect was standing, Cassius repositioned himself to shield Ambivulus from the direction of any new oncoming arrows. Suddenly, as their view cleared, the two Zealots became a half dozen men charging down the sandy slope toward them, dodging pine and olive tree branches as they ran. The Zealots' lone archer was desperately trying to locate a new target as he ran down the hill behind his companions on the left.

Cassius realized that as soon as the Zealots reached the clearing, they would try to move between Cassius and Bracus, separating them on opposite sides of the brook.

Cassius looked at his prefect and shouted, "Sir, stay here. Bracus, up the slope on your right, I'll come from the left!" Then Cassius took off at a run. He turned just once to confirm Bracus was running up the slope, using the blooming olive trees as cover.

Pumping his legs hard, Cassius tore up the eastern hillside toward the Zealots. '*Move faster, move!*' he screamed inside his head. Arm raised, sword in hand, he knew his first real combat was imminent.

The first Zealot, armed with both a javelin and a short sword, yelled to intimidate his approaching Roman target. He then contorted his torso to launch his javelin toward Cassius.

With a quick swing of his sword, Cassius ricocheted the spear off to his right. The Zealot pulled his sword from his belt, still running downhill toward him.

Cassius's training took control of his movements. He raised his own sword in a defensive move, perpendicular to his head and shoulders. The approaching Zealot raised his sword overhead and leaped to strike.

Then Cassius did something his opponent had not expected. He twisted his shoulders and threw his sword at the man, striking the Zealot in the right shoulder. The man yelled in pain and dropped his sword. He hobbled sideways and slipped on the loose rocks. As the Zealot slid down the hill, Cassius kicked and knocked the man unconscious.

Cassius turned and grabbed the sword of the fallen Zealot and swung it across the outstretched body of the second Zealot who had followed his companion down the hill. The slicing blow knocked him backward. The maneuver gave Cassius time to steady himself for more fighting. The long hours of intense combat training had generated lethal, instinctual responses in him. A second thrust from Cassius impaled the Zealot in the abdomen. Cassius turned, looking for immediate danger and his next opponent.

Across the clearing, Cassius saw Bracus running desperately at two Zealots. Like Cassius's first assailant, the nearest Zealot was armed with a javelin and lunged at Bracus. Bracus parleyed with his sword as the Zealot approached, deflecting the iron spearhead and burying it into the ground as it glanced off his shin guard. Bracus raised his sword and cut across his attacker's torso in one continuous motion, breaking his shoulder and carving a deep wound in the man's chest.

Cassius continued to look around for the archer. From the corner of his eye, he saw Bracus turn to meet the second Zealot. In his right hand, he picked up the first Zealot's javelin. Cassius recalled his sergeant's training. *"Be careful how you aim. The weapon you throw can become the one that kills you!"*

The Zealot stopped short when he saw Bracus holding the javelin in his right hand and a sword in his left.

Cassius pulled his attention away from Bracus when he found the lone archer up the hill, feet braced, drawing back his bow to launch another arrow aimed directly at Prefect Ambivulus.

Cassius screamed, "Arrow!" in the direction of the prefect. The arrow flew past Cassius to an empty space where the prefect had stood a second earlier and embedded in a tree.

Using the olive trees for cover, Cassius started running uphill toward the archer. He was desperate to reach the Zealot before he could notch another arrow. Then from the corner of his eye, Cassius sighted Marcus Ambivulus who had already circled up the hill and was approaching the archer from above, sword in hand.

Facing three Roman soldiers, the remaining three Zealots looked at each other, one gave a shout in Aramaic and ran back up the hill with Bracus in pursuit.

"Bracus, stop!" Cassius called out. "Protect the prefect first. Get our horses!"

Cassius turned to Prefect Ambivulus, who nodded his approval. All three headed down to the edge of the olive grove, where the horses were tied, with Bracus limping behind. At the bottom of the hill, Cassius looked up at Bracus as he hobbled down the hill, his right leg bleeding from the deflected javelin. *'Father would be proud of us today, Bracus. We've become real soldiers.'*

Saddling and then mounting their startled horses, the threesome galloped back to Fortress Antonia. Prefect Ambivulus laughed, exhilarated to be in combat again, away from the senseless politics of Judea. Cassius and Bracus were stunned by the events of the day. Finding out their father was a hero! And they had just fought their first real battle. Now they were true soldiers!

REMEMBERING OLD BATTLE LINES

"Silus, it was like Germania. Quintus's boys fought like seasoned soldiers. Cassius put himself in harm's way to shield me from attack." Marcus was breathing hard retelling his story to his tribune and friend.

Silus could only shake his head, smile, then grimace. Still, he was irritated at his superior officer, the governor of Judea and Samaria, and his friend.

"I told you Quintus had trained them well. Now, can you explain why you were galloping outside of Jerusalem without at least a full squad of cavalry? There are six thousand soldiers and cavalrymen in the fortress, and you chose to ride out with two guards you happened to pick up along the way? Don't you think that a bit foolhardy?"

"Don't quibble with details, Silus! I want those boys promoted. From what little information I got from Cassius, I'd say they are better educated than most of our officers."

"As long as you don't venture alone outside of Jerusalem again! You know the Zealots have been looking for a reason to start a revolution. But before promotions, let's see how far Quintus has taken their education."

"All right, test the boys. I've seen them ride; they should be in the cavalry. Cassius said Quintus taught them archery as well. That can easily be established. These two boys could be a decade beyond their peers. We need good officers who can think and fight to keep the peace in Judea. I don't care how old they are!"

As Prefect Ambivulus walked out of his friend's apartment, still breathing hard from the excitement, he looked back. "I know they will surprise you."

Chapter 3

SOMETHING GAINED, SOMETHING LOST

16 AD

FORTRESS ANTONIA

"Out of your cots, you lazy rats!" screamed the centurion. Six days after the encounter with the Zealots, Tribune Valens and Centurion Clavius Orestes walked into Cassius's barrack an hour before dawn.

The one hundred men sleeping in their cots awakened to the sounds of Centurion Orestes kicking loose helmets and buckets through the rows of sleeping soldiers. Cassius and Bracus looked up to a dim torchlight approaching them. Two ominous figures walked beside the torch: legion officers.

"Cassius, Bracus, you have three minutes to get dressed and armored. Meet me before I lose my temper, or you'll be swabbing sh*t buckets for a month!"

Stumbling out of their cots, the two young soldiers recognized Tribune Valens standing next to their centurion. Cassius immediately assumed they had done something horribly wrong, severe enough to be punished in front of the rest of the legion. Running as fast as they could, the pair gathered clothes and armor and ran to the front of the barrack door, where Centurion Orestes waited with folded arms and an unwelcoming scowl.

Frantically arranging their armor chest plates, swords, and shields, Cassius and Bracus jumped outside to find two saddled garrison horses waiting for them. The centurion ordered them to mount the horses.

"Carry on, Orestes," Valens instructed, and he turned and walked back toward his apartment in the fortress.

Centurion Orestes nodded, mounted, and rode off with Cassius and Bracus in tow. A few minutes later they arrived at the prefect's palace. "Dismount and report to Master Claudius Agrippa and obey his commands!" Centurion Orestes ordered. Without further comment, he turned and rode away.

Cassius tied his horse to a rail, looked at Bracus, and shrugged. Bracus looked bewildered. Cassius led the way as they walked past the guards, who in turn gave them awkward stares. Entering the palace, Cassius found a young servant woman and asked where Master Agrippa's apartment was located. She pointed toward a corner of the palace and quickly ran down the opposite hallway. Again, Cassius looked at Bracus and shrugged.

Entering the apartment, Cassius looked around the dimly lit room and found an old man with a long grey beard sitting next to a small wooden table with a half-empty bowl of porridge and dates. Claudius Agrippa was leaning back on a wooden chair, head resting on the wall of the room, eyes closed.

Bracus turned to Cassius. "Maybe he's asleep. We could be off the hook."

But Claudius rose at the sound, muttered an obscenity, and barked at Cassius and Bracus to sit down at the long table.

"You've ruined a perfectly good morning!" Claudius gave them hardened stares as if he were about to slaughter them like a chicken and dress them for roasting.

Laying two sets of parcels and scribes before him, the prefect's Master of Education began grilling the boys on history, politics, and Greek. Then he made them demonstrate their mathematical knowledge, solving a series of problems on the blank parcels.

Though it was cool in the apartment, Cassius noticed that Bracus was sweating. His answers, though adequate, were getting slower and less precise. As Bracus continued to delay, Claudius became even more angry and impatient. It became obvious that Claudius was determined to reduce the two farm boys to well-deserved and proper humiliation.

While Bracus struggled for answers, they miraculously always seemed to come. Unaware of the depth of the men's friendship, Claudius was completely blind to the subtle signals Cassius provided Bracus during the examination. Finally, after four hours and what seemed an eternity, the drills ended.

Grey-haired, wrinkled, his voice hoarse, Claudius shouted, "Enough! Go back to your barracks!" He picked up a wooden straw broom and held it with an iron grip, like a weapon. His distorted face broadcast obvious frustration.

Cassius turned to question Claudius about why they'd been sent to him. But the old man only glared at him and then angrily started sweeping the floor.

On the way back, Cassius mounted his horse and looked at Bracus. His friend kept his head low as he wheeled his horse around to return to the fortress. Bracus immediately spurred his horse into a canter.

Once out of hearing range from the prefect's palace, Bracus shot an angry barrage of questions at Cassius. "What was that all about? We didn't join the Legion to be tested in mathematics, Greek, and history! What did we do wrong?"

"I'm not sure. Maybe they have plans for us we aren't aware of?" responded Cassius, controlling his frustration for his friend's sake.

"Maybe we'll be punished for being presumptuous to Prefect Ambivulus? And we've missed breakfast and any chance for lunch," complained Bracus.

Cassius saw hunger and fear on Bracus's face. He knew Bracus always tended toward the extreme when tired and hungry, allowing his worst fears to take control. Cassius couldn't respond—nothing would make it better for Bracus except returning to their routine and a meal.

Cassius was more hopeful when he considered the day's events. Clearly, they had been punished as arrogant young soldiers who needed lessons in humility. Perhaps they would face double guard duty or forced marching around the fortress. That wasn't so bad.

When they arrived back at Fortress Antonia, Tribune Valens and Centurion Orestes were waiting for them. Their grim faces portrayed no emotion as the centurion ordered, "Cassius, Bracus, return to your normal duties. Report to your sergeant."

Cassius thought he would test his luck. "Sir, we haven't eaten today. Can we swing by the kitchens first?"

"Go on, make it quick. Now out of here!" ordered the centurion.

Cassius was thankful for the quick meal, both for his empty stomach and for the sake of Bracus. Spending the rest of the day with a hungry and frustrated Bracus did not appeal to him in the least. Cassius had always felt responsible for Bracus. It was his duty to look after him.

He had to find out the reason behind Master Agrippa's interrogation, if for nothing else but Bracus's piece of mind. Cassius made plans to corner the centurion after the evening meal, hoping to get an explanation for the morning's events.

The rest of the day was uneventful except for occasional curious stares from fellow soldiers. By the end of the evening meal, Cassius was getting more and more frustrated. No one seemed able to explain the unusual events of the morning. Then he spied Centurion Orestes in the dining hall and took his chance. Cassius jumped up from the remnants of his meal and walked toward the centurion. Just as he had cleared his table, Cassius heard a shuffle behind him and realized that Bracus was in close pursuit.

As the pair approached Centurion Orestes, Tribune Valens walked up to the threesome.

"Orestes, please take these soldiers to your office. I'll be there in five minutes," Valens instructed.

Cassius stood at attention with Bracus in their centurion's office, waiting for their punishment. A few moments later, Tribune Valens entered the room and handed Cassius and Bracus a parcel with the prefect's seal.

Cassius looked up and saw smirking eyes behind the otherwise cold expressions of their tribune and centurion.

"Starting tomorrow, you two will be promoted to Avocati soldiers with appropriate pay raises. You've demonstrated expert fighting skills with the sword and lance, ride horses like you were born on them, and evidently have an uncommon education." Valens's voice betrayed his pride in the boys as he informed them of their promotions.

Tribune Valens continued, "I'm not sure how you frustrated Claudius Agrippa's attempts to confirm that you are the idiots he believed, but somehow, he couldn't find fault with your answers. He now claims you are possessed by demons and demands that both of you be crucified."

Valens paused to let Agrippa's request sink in. "Thankfully, Prefect Ambivulus calmed him down. The prefect told Master Agrippa that your education was provided by a master educator over many years, starting at birth. Ironically, the prefect seems to know more about you two than your centurion does."

Tribune Valens continued, "I've discussed this with your centurion at length and he assures me he'll be exploring the depth of your talents. When you see Prefect Ambivulus next time, be sure to thank him for saving your lives from crucifixion."

Centurion Orestes smiled and announced, "Congratulations! You are years ahead of your peers. Now both of you are dismissed. Go celebrate and try not to kill yourselves tonight. Your promotion starts tomorrow."

Cassius smiled and looked at Bracus, whose mouth hung open, his eyes bulging. Cassius gave Bracus a quick stab in the ribs with his elbow to nudge his friend back to reality.

"Thank you, sir!" Cassius exclaimed as he saluted. He grabbed Bracus by the tunic and dragged him out of the centurion's office.

ZEALOTS

Six months later, Sergeant Cassius Dias was assigned to lead his seventh patrol just outside the gates of Jerusalem. Just prior to the patrol, Centurion Orestes pulled Cassius aside.

"Cassius, Jews are continuing to harass Roman patrols. We have a spy who tells us about a small Zealot troop gathering in the area east of the city. Their meeting on the Sabbath is a mistake. The Jews don't expect our patrols tonight, thinking that we'll stand down for their Sabbath. Just in case, Tribune Valens ordered five patrols of the area, each with a dozen soldiers. You'll lead the patrol just southeast of the city. I've given you Sergeant Bracus for extra support."

"Yes sir," Cassius replied. "If we encounter Zealots, do we arrest them?"

"Yes, if you can. If they resist, protect your men first."

Cassius nodded, raised his right arm to his chest in salute, and returned to the barracks to brief his men.

As dusk crept over Jerusalem, Cassius and his patrol walked out of Fortress Antonia. Lanterns were lit in the small homes and larger estates of the city as businesses were closed tight to begin the Sabbath at sundown. They heard Sabbath prayers as they passed homes on their way to the south gate. They could also smell the aromas of the Sabbath meal, lamb and chicken being roasted on open pits.

Leaving the city, they began long hours of searching, finally arriving at the outermost edge of their search area.

"So, the centurion chose you again to lead us on a goose chase. Better not screw this patrol up, Cassius. You'll be under my command next time." Bracus smiled, his words meant to prod Cassius out of his fatigue.

"For that comment, Bracus, you'll have the pleasure of being point-man for the remainder of the night!" laughed Cassius, now fully awake. He knew on the next patrol that Bracus led, there would be payback.

Arriving at a seemingly deserted building on the north corner of a dead olive grove, Cassius instructed Bracus and two fellow soldiers to search the building and surrounding area. Bracus cautiously walked toward a dilapidated farm building. As he approached the building, he heard what sounded like surprised and agitated men scrambling for their weapons. Seconds later, twenty Zealots poured from the building, armed with short battle swords and strung bows with notched arrows.

Standing in front of the Roman torches, Bracus's silhouette was clearly defined for the Zealot archers. A moment later, six Zealot arrows launched toward the nearest three Romans: Bracus and his men.

As the arrows whizzed by Cassius, he chuckled at their poor aim. But just as quickly as they had started their escape, half of the Zealots turned, steadied, and aimed their bows. Another barrage of ten arrows flew in the direction of Bracus and his two companions.

The soldiers scrambled for any cover they could find. Bracus, being ahead of the two soldiers, stood out as a clear target. Arrows flew; this time their track was true.

Bracus staggered backward as the first arrow struck his chest, just above his left breast plate, a second to his right arm. Gurgling blood from his mouth, Bracus groaned, searching for Cassius, his eyes pleading for help.

Hearing the shouts of the advance guard, Cassius screamed orders to his men.

"Archery formation now!" Standing ahead of his men, he watched as his soldiers formed a half-dome defensive formation. Shields forward and interlocking, Cassius was satisfied his men could protect themselves from any subsequent incoming arrows.

"Move forward, toward the building!" Cassius's next order was to provide protection for Bracus and his companions.

"Bracus, Anthony, Tavian! Stay low, we are coming for you!" Cassius cried. In response, Zealots screamed orders to each other and ran directly toward the Roman formation. Then they turned and quickly formed rough battle lines, replacing arrows on their bows.

"These rebels are soldiers! Charge them!" Cassius yelled to his men, hoping to reach the Zealots before they could organize further.

In the confused melee, Cassius stood alone, dodging arrows and spiked javelins. He knew he had to keep his men moving forward in formation. He caught sight of a familiar shape lying on the ground, holding an arrow in his chest.

"Bracus! I'm coming!" Cassius ran toward the end of the Zealots' line, making a path directly for Bracus. Two

Zealots ran to intercept Cassius, confronting him with swords and javelins.

Enraged, Cassius raised his own sword to thwart a javelin thrust toward his stomach. Spinning to his right, he used his left hand to shove his javelin into the throat of the second Zealot. The wounded man shrank to the ground, holding onto the javelin. Cassius twisted around again, throwing his sword into the shoulder of the remaining Zealot.

Picking up the dying man's sword, Cassius continued running toward Bracus. But before he could reach his friend, he slowed, quietly recognizing the brutality of Bracus's wounds.

Turning toward his men, he saw that the fighting had become close combat. He ignored the combat and finally reached Bracus. Kneeing down, he cradled Bracus's head and wrapped his arms around his chest.

Bracus's breathing grew shorter, tighter. Each subsequent breath seemed to become more difficult, wheezing small gasps of air.

Bracus had begun his journey to Elysium. Racing thoughts began to slow time itself as Cassius recognized the signs of imminent death. He held Bracus even tighter, as though he could prevent the inevitable. In one final gesture, Bracus gripped Cassius's hand and whispered, ". . . not alone."

As death stole Bracus, silence created an abyss between the friends. Time became irrelevant. Overwhelmed, Cassius raged against the loss of his childhood companion, his brother. There was no good to be found in this man's death. Bracus was gone.

Bearing his loss alone, Cassius screamed again in agony. Then he stood up to take his revenge. He transformed from a soldier to a hunter. The Jews weren't subjects to be controlled—they were murderers to be punished.

Cassius surveyed the ongoing fight. His men were surrounded, fighting desperately for their lives. Cassius felt as though he was dreaming. He looked down and saw his own legs running back to the fight. He no longer heard his screams or felt his rage. He was only action.

Switching his sword to his left hand, Cassius dislodged his javelin from the dead Zealot without slowing down. He found himself in the center of the Zealot soldiers. His heart was pounding so hard and fast that he could hear the beats in his head, reminding him of the battle cadence of the Roman drummers during their practice. Time slowed further and he watched himself become a lethal weapon.

Cassius threw his javelin, impaling a rebel in the stomach. The man staggered, falling to the ground, mouthing a silent scream. Picking up another short sword, Cassius continued to the next Zealot. He watched as the Zealot pulled an arrow from his quiver, turned, and pointed a half-cocked arrow at him.

Cassius responded by throwing his short sword at the rebel, which glanced off the archer's shoulder with enough force to make him lose his cocked arrow from his bow. Cassius launched another attack with his remaining sword, cutting the archer through his leather armor. The Zealot simply slumped down onto the waiting ground.

Cassius looked around to see the battle continue in slow motion. In an uncontrolled rage, he continued, picking up the archer's bow, taking the quiver, notching arrows, and releasing strike after strike against the Zealots.

The next recipient was a rebel in the process of raising his sword to strike a Roman soldier who had fallen. The arrow caught the Zealot in the armpit, driving the shaft deep into the man's heart. He fell without a noise.

Cassius looked down and saw blood on his hands. Bracus's blood. "My god," he swore, "do not let me lose another brother tonight!"

Cassius mechanically notched the next arrow, fired, and immediately notched another before he saw the effect of the first. A Zealot fell to his knees, an arrow protruding out of his lower back.

Continuing to launch arrows, Cassius struck another Zealot in the leg and fatally wounded another with a strike to the neck.

Then, as suddenly as the battle had started, it was over. His soldiers had done their duty. Of the twenty rebels, only two remained to flee, three more that lay in the orchard clearing were too severely wounded to move.

As the adrenaline of the battle faded, exhaustion and despair set in. Bracus was gone. Cassius stumbled over to his friend's body, knelt, and unleashed tears that rolled off his cheeks onto Bracus's lifeless body.

"Bracus, stay with me." Cassius pleaded one last time, as though he could change reality and make his friend hear him. After long moments of mourning, Cassius slowly lifted Bracus's body into his arms and began the long return to Fortress Antonia. Stoically walking past the silent carnage of the battlefield, Cassius kept his eyes forward, afraid to look down at Bracus lest he collapses into the depths of his loss.

As he passed his soldiers, each lifted their right arm to their chest, a final salute.

The death of Bracus, his brother, burnt deep within Cassius. Guilt encapsulated his shame, a shame that nurtured a dark uncertainty about life itself.

As Cassius sank deeper into the wretched reality of this day, one truth was certain: Bracus was gone. He wondered how he could ever fathom a life of peace or joy again. Pain overwhelmed hope.

Chapter 4

SARA'S MIRACLE

17 AD
JERUSALEM

Sara's lips drew tight, the wrinkles around her eyes more pronounced than usual. She held the washcloth tightly in her hands, as tightly as she held a secret. Her anxiety had reached a climax; tonight, she had to reconcile the truth. For a month she had lived hanging onto a nagging suspicion, ignoring obvious signs. After consulting with several of her friends, all midwives, she knew she had to face the growing truth inside her. She was pregnant again.

She weighed the years that she and Joseph had prayed for more children. Each time they ignored the additional cost and responsibilities. Sara acknowledged their son, Jonathan, had been a blessing. But now he was coming to the age of maturity. At twelve, Jonathan had already performed his first Alayah in the Temple last month. Sara felt as though the family was beginning to shrink as Jonathan grew and became more independent.

Joseph had always felt it wasn't right to leave Jonathan without siblings. Years ago, Sara agreed that if God provided them with another child, it would be a blessing. But over the years, she became discouraged that perhaps there would be no more children in their future. If there was any solace in her thoughts, it was that God was looking out for them—the additional mouth to feed might have been a burden too hard to carry.

Yet, now, a simple but unexpected miracle had occurred. Her hopes and prayers turned to doubt and fear. For the first time, she wondered how Joseph would receive the news. She feared the additional responsibility might unsettle their lives, just as they had finally found a small measure of peace.

For years, Joseph had consistently looked for jobs, finding temporary work as a carpenter. Their security was elusive until Joseph was able to establish himself as a carpenter for the new temple. The Pharisees were pleased with his craftsmanship and promised him work for years to come. Sara appreciated the routine in their life. The additional money Sara earned by sewing and mending clothes allowed them to eat a little better than they had in years.

When Jonathan joined his father as an apprentice carpenter, Sara was overjoyed. Joseph loved to have Jonathan working with him. He was a patient teacher, much like his own father who had taught him the trade many years prior.

In turn, Sara saw the joy Jonathan experienced learning to become a carpenter, just like his father. She had always been amazed to see the love her husband put into his work, seeing a job done with patience and quality. Now her son was slowly being shaped into the image of his father, and Sara carried her pride as she tended the house.

It was dusk when Sara heard Joseph enter their small house on the outskirts of Jerusalem. Today it had been especially hot in the Temple, and she knew Joseph looked forward to a cool sanctuary after his hard labor of the day. Sara smiled as she saw Jonathan trailing behind, a sweating, dirty mess.

"Your dinners are on the table. We have treats tonight. Lamb, olives, pickled vegetables, and bread. And honeyed figs for dessert if you can find room." Sara saw the quizzical look on Joseph's face. Lamb was not a typical meal, either for a normal day or the Sabbath, and the figs signaled that something was amiss.

Oblivious, Jonathan just screeched in delight as he began to wash after the long day.

"You both have worked so hard today," Sara said in defense.

The look Joseph gave her told her he wasn't fooled, but she was thankful he said nothing. For the time Joseph would respect Sara's meal and learn later what was on her mind.

"First wash yourselves. I won't have Temple dust on my dinner table!"

Sara's look directed Joseph to the wash basin. After giving thanks to God, the meal was consumed without unnecessary talk, respecting the special treat. Sara smiled as she gazed at both Joseph and Jonathan, soaking their bread in the fat drippings of the lamb.

The most precious gifts of life were sitting before her. Joseph and Jonathan leaned back on their pillows, completely at ease with the world in this moment. Jonathan's grin from the meal was notched into his face. His cheeks began to ache from the laughter, grins, and special food.

Suddenly, Sara felt the pang of remorse that she would interrupt their bliss with news that would likely shake their foundations. Joseph was going to be a father again. Jonathan was going to be a brother.

Sara broke the indulging silence. "Jonathan, we need more water to clean. Can you go to the well and bring us another jar?"

Sara noticed Joseph's eyes light up. He knew she always gathered sufficient water for the house in the mornings. Jonathan hesitated briefly then unwound himself from the dinner table, getting up with a groan, and then ran off on his errand.

Joseph started the conversation. "Sara, what is it?"

Sara started to cry and blurted out, "Joseph, God has given us a gift and a burden. After all these years of waiting," she sighed, then took a deep breath, "I'm pregnant."

She watched as Joseph's mouth dropped open. She could tell he was trying to absorb the surprise. Fearing his rejection, Sara sobbed, tears rolling down her tanned cheeks until they reached her trembling mouth.

She couldn't know that Joseph's mind was racing in another time, another place. Inside, he was screaming for joy, thrust back to the time when Jonathan was born. His visions were so real, as though he were there again. Joseph saw himself and the midwives congratulating him on his new son. Then he remembered the love he saw in a small, wrinkled newborn, waving his small arms at his father. Jonathan was crying as loud as his immature lungs could, announcing his arrival into the family. Then Joseph remembered, as he picked up his son, how his legs had buckled and he dropped to his knees, crying. He lifted his head and started to pray, thanking God for the miracle He had given them.

Sara saw Joseph's face distort as he tried to talk. But at that moment, his mouth was broken, useless as a means of communicating. Emotions overwhelmed the reality of the moment. He reached over to Sara and picked her up, gently squeezing her, reassuring her that his covenant with her was unshakable, as was his love.

Feeling Joseph's big hands around her shoulders, and feeling his tears mix with her own, Sara knew that Joseph would love the new child with all his heart and be thankful for God's gift. Sara began to sink in relief, understanding she was truly blessed with the love of this man, their son, and the new child.

Jonathan was running back from the well when he saw his father and mother in a gentle embrace. His joy became concern when he saw the tears in his parents' eyes. Sara reached over to Jonathan and explained, "Son, we are celebrating tonight because next year you will be a big brother."

THE INN

Outside the small home, Joseph stood in the cool night air and prayed, "God of Moses and Abraham, my heart is joyful, yet I am afraid. How can I support my growing family? How can we provide for this new child?"

'Where will the money come from to support my family? Can I keep them safe from the dangers of Roman occupation, Herod's taxes, and Zealot resistance?'

"My God, my wages are meager, and taxes ruthless. We are but a simple people. We ask for your help," Joseph prayed.

After returning to the house, Joseph found Sara in bed, physically and emotionally drained from the meal preparations and anxiety over her news. Jonathan had been sent to bed to rest before tomorrow's work. After sitting quietly in the dark house, on the black moonless night, Joseph quietly slipped out of the house.

Still awake, Sara recognized the mixture of both joy and fear in Joseph. She allowed her husband the illusion that he was leaving the small, thatched house unnoticed. She also knew where he was going and smiled. As Sara lay in bed, she shared the same fears as Joseph and prayed for both her husband and unborn child. Finally, after several hours of praying and crying, she yielded to common sense and awakened Jonathan to bring her husband back from his night of celebration at Staff and Sword Inn.

"After a few drinks, your father feels like he's best friends with everyone in Jerusalem. His heart is truly made from the love of God, but sometimes we need him back on this earth. He has work tomorrow and must get some sleep."

Jonathan smiled and nodded sleepily. As he left the house, Sara called out, "Jonathan, be careful, avoid groups and soldiers in the alleys!"

Silently, Jonathan traveled through the streets of Jerusalem to Staff and Sword Inn. As he approached the Inn, Jonathan could hear his father's exuberant voice.

"To the glory of God! Another child!"

Peering inside the tavern doors, Jonathan looked around to see his father in the corner of the Inn, raising a toast with his friends. Standing beside the doorway, Jonathan dared not speak, so he simply waited for his father's attention, witnessing his father's joy.

HEROD ANTIPAS

Afraid of Zealots and thieves, Herod consistently blamed the lack of Roman protection for his insecurities and demanded additional Roman soldiers to supplement his guards. He also blamed the Romans for the very existence of the Zealot rebels. After all, he rationalized, if the Romans had left Judea to the Jews, there wouldn't be a need for Zealots.

But Herod was also shrewd, his actions politically driven, even when it came to his family. In truth, Herod Antipas desperately desired to become the King of all Judea, Samaria, and the surrounding provinces. He yearned for the respect and admiration that his father, Herod the Great, had commanded but had always lacked his father's strength and wisdom.

Sitting in his throne room, Herod laughed and looked at his kitchen master.

"Chuza, once more we have outwitted the dull Marcus Ambivulus. He gave in to my demands for more Roman guards. I told him I needed extra guards because of the Zealots. It was so easy. I blamed them for the unrest. Now he's given us leverage to use his soldiers whenever we need them. It was a mistake on Marcus's part. Next, we'll ask for permanent

Roman guards here in the palace. Again, the unrest will be their fault. Once Ambivulus leaves and is replaced by another prefect, the precedent will be cast in stone. Ha!"

Chuza listened but did not comment.

"I can still be the King of Judea and Samaria. I just need to maneuver Rome to give up Judea. The rest will fall under my authority!"

Herod Antipas laughed again, then investigated his cup as he took another large gulp of wine to celebrate his supposed victory over Prefect Ambivulus.

CASSIUS

Bracus's death still weighed heavily on Cassius's mind. And it changed everything. Isolated in Jerusalem, far from his family and friends in Tuscany, Cassius felt alone.

More importantly, Cassius was ashamed and angry at himself. His father was able to protect his best friend in Germania, turning away hordes of Gauls, but Cassius couldn't even protect Bracus from a rabble of Zealots. He feared the day he would have to face his father and explain how Bracus died. But in the meantime, he kept to himself and his duties. He believed that to protect his soldiers, he had to become stronger and smarter. Although Cassius had written to his family about Bracus, he had not communicated with them since. He just wanted to be alone to face his shame.

Three months after the ambush, Cassius had been transferred to King Herod's guards. There he found that he had more free time to push himself harder. Remaining aloof,

Cassius chose to train alone, unless his exercises required sparring partners for sword or javelin practice. To avoid thinking about Bracus, Cassius had become a driven man. It wasn't long before his life solely focused on his duties as a soldier, any spare time dedicated to a regimen of rigorous exercise.

By the end of the first year of guard duty in Herod's palace, his routine had bled into endless days of monotony, exacerbated by a dry, hot summer. By August, the infrequent cooling breeze from the west had gone, leaving Jerusalem with sweltering days of heat and dryness. The only respite against the monotony was the fact that Cassius had been promoted to standard.

By the middle of August, Herod started using his Roman guards to escort himself, his wife Phasaelis, and his guests to cool areas outside the city. Herod demanded extra guards from Prefect Ambivulus for these outings, to protect his wife and ladies of the court in case of Zealot attacks. Once again, Marcus Ambivulus acquiesced to appease Herod rather than escalate a political fight that could reach the halls of Rome.

Cassius soon found that guarding King Herod and his family had become harder. As Herod, his wife, and guests ate fresh fruit and bread under the shade of Gethsemane cypress and olive trees; Cassius and his squadron of six Roman guards remained by the roadside, void of any shelter or shade. The only provisions for the day were the hardened bread and warm water they carried.

By late afternoon, the family was escorted back to the palace to find respite within the shaded marble walls and floors. But once again, the guards stood in the heat of the palace. Occasionally, Master Chuza, Herod's kitchen manager, brought out fresh water and fruit for the guards, but only when Herod had left the palace. Today, Herod was inside with his family, and there were no kitchen refreshments.

Today their guard watch went into the evening. Herod's family was once again enjoying an abundant meal in their cooled dining area.

Finally, Cassius and his men were relieved, all dog-tired as they marched into Fortress Antonia. They were thirsty, hungry, and dirty from the sweat generated by hours in the sun, their only shade the rolling dust from the eastern winds that covered their bodies.

"To the bathhouse and bathe off today's stench," he ordered. "After that, we'll see what's left in the dining hall."

After bathing off the grime, Cassius led his men to the massive dining hall. By the time they entered, lined with enough long tables and stools to seat thousands, it was already two hours past the last call for supper. The kitchens were closed; little food or wine remained. Still, Cassius hoped for the best. Unfortunately, he found only pots of tepid gruel left over from lunch, more hard stale bread, and wine that tasted more like vinegar.

As he seated himself at an empty table, Cassius tried to get the tasteless gruel past his mouth, hoping to somehow bypass his taste buds. He soon heard three of his soldiers call out to him.

"Standard, Cassius, join us! We're going to get something to drink besides this swill."

Cassius didn't respond.

"It was unbearably hot today; we need decent food and good wine!"

"Can you please get us out of the fort tonight?" begged Lucius.

Cassius turned on his stool and nudged the gruel and the vinegar-wine away. Frustrated, he made the decision not to go to bed hungry again. He looked up at his men, "I can't argue with you. But just two drinks. Tomorrow will be another hard day."

He ordered his men to arm themselves with swords. They marched outside the fortress's front gate as though they were on their way to relieve guards in Herod's palace. Then Cassius and his companions headed toward the inner markets of Jerusalem and to the center of town.

It was a 30-minute walk through the streets of Jerusalem. Approaching Staff and Sword Inn well past sunset, Cassius felt that the August day had not been cooled by the coming of night and the dryness in the air was such to drive any man to a deep thirst. Though the four soldiers were more thirsty than hungry, they still looked forward to a decent meal of chicken and vegetables. Arriving at Staff and Sword Inn, they were surprised by the sounds of celebrating customers inside the tavern.

JONATHAN

Jonathan stood in the doorway, watching his father inside the inn, when four large figures approached him from behind. The first man moved around Jonathan, but the three other men brushed him aside as they tried to gain access to the inn simultaneously. Jonathan looked up and saw a tall, muscular Roman soldier, leading three shorter but similarly stout soldiers.

Afraid to respond to their rudeness, Jonathan said nothing. Recovering his balance, he leaned against the door again, concerned that Roman soldiers entering the inn could mean trouble.

He wanted to call out to his father, but instead, he waved. Watching the soldiers bump and jar customers as they headed for a table, Jonathan's fears subsided a bit as the soldiers sat down at the table and waved to the innkeeper. Perhaps there would be no trouble tonight after all.

JOSEPH

Joseph's laughter and salutations subsided with the entrance of the soldiers. He turned his head, gazing at Jonathan with the pride of a father. He smiled at his son, and in his drunken state, began to weep with joy mixed with the fear of the hardened life his family endured. He winked at his son and raised his hand to indicate he would be with him in one moment.

Joseph rose and started to walk across the crowded tavern. As he approached the table of Romans, one of the soldiers extended his leg to trip Joseph. Falling forward, Joseph landed on the Roman table, spilling wine onto the soldier who'd tripped him.

Joseph lurched backward, standing upright, surprised and embarrassed. He looked directly at the soldier, the tallest one who had led the group in, and staggered upright, stuttering a few mutilated words to apologize. In response, the soldier stood up and loosened his dagger as a precaution.

Cassius, standing and watching the man carefully, thought this drunken Jew's 'accident' might be a prelude to an attack. He slowly moved around the table.

Joseph lurched backward in a second attempt to stand up. By extending his muscled arms to balance himself, he landed against an adjacent table and rebounded away from the soldiers.

"Joseph, you drunken fool, go celebrate with your wife and son!" John, the blacksmith, shouted from the adjacent table. He laughed and pushed Joseph forward.

Joseph stumbled and fell forward, directly into Cassius's unsheathed dagger. Falling back to John's table, Joseph clutched his abdomen with a look of surprise and horror.

It was only a few seconds before the stain of blood had drenched his garment. Joseph's eyes widened with surprise at the sharp pain in his stomach, his inability to speak, and his weakening legs that buckled underneath him. Thinking of Sara, Joseph fell to the floor. He looked for Jonathan across the room and found his son staring at him with disbelief and horror.

Cassius staggered back and stared at the blood on his dagger with equal surprise. He swore at Joseph for his stupidity. Yet the hollow look in Cassius's eyes betrayed his fear: had he gone too far, reacted too quickly? But it wasn't the time to show weakness to the Jews. Roman weakness would not be tolerated.

Across the room, Jonathan watched the surreal events unfolding. Time and reality shut down. Was it possible? Could he believe his eyes? Certainly, this was a trick, a cruel stunt played at the expense of a crying twelve-year-old boy. But the gathering crowd around his father proved otherwise.

Rushing to his father, Jonathan lay his head on his father's shoulder, tears rolling from his face onto his dirty cheeks. Motionless, Joseph was unable to reassure Jonathan, so he closed his eyes to avoid seeing his son crying over him, Jonathan's face convulsing as he gasped for air.

Moments later, John lay a huge hand on Jonathan's shoulder and stated the horrible truth that others could already see for themselves. "Jonathan, your father is gone." Jonathan made one last attempt to awaken his father from his death sleep. Grabbing Joseph's tunic, Jonathan tried to lift his father to stand. Not able to bear the weight of his father, Jonathan fell backward into the arms of John. Speechless, John wrapped his huge blacksmith arms around Jonathan and cried with him.

MARY

Nahum gripped Mary's forearm tighter. Mary looked up and started to struggle when she saw the palace of Herod Antipas. As they approached the palace side door, she began to protest.

"Uncle Nahum, please! I will work past sunset on the farm! Please don't sell me." Without support from relatives, Mary faced an unacceptable choice: become a street prostitute or be indentured as a palace maid.

Uncle Nahum made the choice for Mary. He chose servitude in the palace of Herod Antipas rather than finding his niece roaming the streets of Magdala. It was the obvious choice. He was a respectable merchant and couldn't endanger his trade, not while he still lived in Magdala.

At the entrance, the palace guard looked upon the approaching pair and lowered his javelin to prevent them from entering.

"I am here to see Chuza, the kitchen master. I'm bringing him a new girl for the kitchens."

The guards looked down on Mary and laughed. "Looks like she is an unwilling wench. Chuza will have his hands full until she is tamed. Go in, I'll send word for him."

Twenty minutes later, Chuza walked up and asked, "Who are you and where are you from?"

"I am Nahum from Magdala, in Galilee. This is Mary. She was thirteen last month. Her parents were killed when the Romans crushed the rebel insurrection last year. They burned her house down with her parents inside. My wife died two months ago and I can't care for her anymore. We have made arrangements for Mary to work here."

Chuza looked down at Mary, quickly recognizing this pretty young girl could have potential in the palace.

Nahum continued, "There is one thing you should know. From time to time, she shakes and then faints. She never harms anyone, nor does she talk in strange tongues. She just faints."

Chuza continued to look at Mary, "Will she work hard?"

"Yes, she is a hard worker and obeys, Master Chuza. She works from dawn to dusk without complaint."

Chuza nodded and pulled a bag of coins from his belt. "Twenty silver shekels due to her shaking."

Nahum grumbled under his breath but took the bag. "Work hard, Mary, and they will not harm you." He walked away and out the gate without looking at her again, clutching his bag of silver.

Mary looked at Chuza and saw the young man staring at her. Barely twenty himself, Chuza had been indentured in the palace since he was a child and was consistently promoted because of his loyalty and hard work. Despite his inclination to show this pretty girl pity, he knew it would only make matters worse for her.

"Come with me, Mary. You'll room with another kitchen girl, Joanna. She will show you your duties. Work hard, stay out of trouble, and you won't be punished. And stay away from the male servants and guards."

Mary arrived at a small door inside the palace. The wooden door opened to a room with six small cots entombed by stucco walls. There was no window, no light. The room was as black as a deep well. Chuza took a lamp off a small table by the door and lit the wick. There were straw baskets for clothes next to the cots and a chamber pot for late-night needs. The room was empty and smelled of filth. Mary felt trapped and started to cry.

'There is no hope,' she thought, *'no one to help or protect me from these Roman barbarians or the palace guards!'*

When Chuza left, Mary made the ultimate decision.

'I'm going to live through this . . .' she promised herself. To survive, her only hope was to make herself plain enough to avoid unwanted attention. She also knew her occasionally epileptic seizures would give her the appearance of an afflicted girl, someone to avoid.

She would bury her natural beauty and easy disposition in quiet solitude. She would wear her hair hidden in a turban and her body in loose clothes to lessen her features and find solace in the mundane.

Mary lay on her cot and wept, tears rolling down her cheeks. Between the gasping for air, she cried. Then Mary did something even she didn't expect. She began to hum a tune in her throat. The tune turned into words and then into song.

She sang the Psalms of her people, asking God for protection. Her soft words were carried by a melodic voice too beautiful to describe. It was as though her voice reverberated through heaven, joined by the angels as she sang the sorrows of man.

Mary was unaware that outside the door stood Joanna, her roommate. As Joanna leaned against the outside wall of their apartment, she listened and began to digest Mary's sorrow. She only had to listen to know the girl's song. Her prayers softened Joanna's heart. Hearing Mary sing, Joanna's mind returned to the first day she became a bonded servant. Fear and loneliness flooded her mind like her first day two years prior, then tears filled the rims of her eyes.

Mary was startled when Joanna entered the room and sat on her cot, directly across from her.

"Please don't stop," Joanna said, eyes reddened by her memories.

Mary hesitated, then continued. Mary's singing touched the soft part of Joanna's soul, that part she had buried to survive in the palace. Then Joanna joined Mary in singing the Psalms. Together, they sang the Lord's song, holding hands and singing prayers of salvation.

Chapter 5

ALONE

22 AD

JERUSALEM

By spring, the markets of Jerusalem were getting full. Merchants were bringing in their best crops in anticipation of the upcoming Passover festival just weeks away. During Passover, hundreds of thousands of Jews were expected to migrate to Jerusalem, doubling the population. Private homes were opened to visitors and relatives. Everywhere the streets of Jerusalem were crowded.

JONATHAN

Jonathan was breathing as hard as he could, pushing his young legs as fast as they could run. The morning rain had created muddy ruts in the streets of Jerusalem, making traction difficult. Sharp turns were hazardous for anyone fleeing, especially from imminent danger. Sliding around street corners, he nearly fell twice. His chest pounded as he sucked in as much air as he could. Just behind Jonathan, four thieves led by the oldest thug named Barabbas, were running hard to catch him.

Turning another corner, Jonathan saw a merchant standing behind a table piled with apples. As Jonathan tripped, he slid in the mud. His only hope of rebounding was to grab the edge of the apple table. As he landed on the next table, onions and cucumbers scattered into the street. Yells and curses followed him as he leaped up to run again, pursuers gaining on him.

Mud now covered Jonathan's legs, tunic, and face. Wiping away splattered filth from his eyes, he looked around the market for his pursuers, desperation carved into his face.

Racing off again, he caught a glimpse of the thugs, thirty yards behind him. Despite the inherent advantage of Jonathan's quickness and flexibility, the mud slowed him down. They were growing still closer.

'You've got to run faster!' he demanded his body to respond.

Several years older and a head taller, the thieves drove their longer legs forward toward their prey. Jonathan clenched his teeth.

'I can't let them catch me . . . I'll be dead if they do.' Jonathan was scared.

Seeing a dark alley behind the Golden Tavern, he thought he could find safety hiding in the shadows. He dashed for the alley. From the corner of his eye, Jonathan saw a man sitting in the back of the alley, directly ahead of him, leaning against a wall, holding a walking shaft. His heavy cloak hid most of his head and shoulders, except for the chiseled features of his face that betrayed a hard life.

'I've seen this beggar before in the eastern marketplace . . . what is he doing here?' Jonathan remembered seeing him hobbling around, barely able to walk.

This man did not look crippled or impaired; there was no despondence on his face. In fact, this stranger was sitting in the alley as if he were expecting Jonathan.

An instant later, the stranger extended his shaft leaning against his shoulder, and caught Jonathan's right ankle, tumbling him forward. Jonathan's arms extended, breaking his fall by his elbows. Despite the surprise, Jonathan tightened his grip on three coins in his right hand. Blood slowly began to flow from both elbows where they'd scraped the ground.

The thieves continued their pursuit, turning into the alley, also gasping for air.

Jonathan watched helplessly as the stranger leaped up and stood in front of him. The thugs stopped. The stranger pulled his cloak back across his waist to expose the foot-long knife in his belt. Two additional men came around the corner to stand behind the stranger and Jonathan. The thieves' anger quickly subsided, replaced with caution, then fear.

"Matthias, we did not know this young pup was under your protection," the oldest thief responded to the stranger's hardened stare.

"We'll take our leave," Barabbas said. They turned and ran out of the alley without looking back.

The two men behind Matthias quietly disappeared. As quickly as the alley pursuit had happened, it was over, and the thieves were gone. Jonathan stood up to face the stranger, his face full of mud and uncertainty.

"What—who are you? Why did you trip me?"

"Quiet, boy," the stranger called Matthias said. "There are important things in the backstreets of this city you are not privy to. For your health, stay where you are." Matthias turned and walked around the corner. Jonathan could hear whispering.

Jonathan began to speak, but Matthias returned with an expression that stopped him cold. "Get up and follow me. Say nothing. Understand?"

Jonathan, confused and disoriented, just looked at Matthias.

Matthias repeated in a harsher, direct voice, "Follow me and don't speak. Understand?" Jonathan nodded.

Moments later, Matthias hustled Jonathan through the city streets, his hood over his head, eyes down, maneuvering through Jerusalem without looking up. Jonathan watched as Matthias occasionally nodded to passing merchants as his pace quickened.

Entering the southern market, they passed through a part of the city alive with merchants calling out to customers, and women haggling over the price of chickens. Jonathan noted that only once did Matthias look back to see if Jonathan was behind him.

Jonathan's mind was racing, trying to clear the adrenalin from his mind and body. '*Who is this man? Why am I following him? Is he going to take my coins and sell me into bondage?*' Jonathan hesitated, pondering his next move. '*I could turn left at the next corner, and he wouldn't notice my absence.*' Yet there was something in the stranger's voice that was not just intimidating but commanding.

'*He ordered me like he knew me,*' Jonathan thought. He watched Matthias's back as he continued his jog through the

city, racing forward to an unknown destination. Jonathan
knew he had to take a chance. His situation was desperate.
He needed help and honest work.

After thirty minutes, they arrived in front of a burnt-out,
vacant inn. The broken shutters and door attested to years of
wanton disregard for necessary repairs.

"In here, Jonathan," ordered Matthias.

Jonathan stopped and stared at the stranger in disbelief.
"You know who I am?"

"Yes. And waiting outside the door is not helping anyone.
Get inside!" barked Matthias. "Go inside. There will be a
woman named Susanna making dinner. Ask her to make us
some soup and we'll talk later."

"But . . ." Jonathan started to reply.

"Go!" barked Matthias and then he disappeared into the
dying light of the day on a retiring Jerusalem.

Jonathan obeyed and entered. The front of the inn had
burned years ago, but the structure was still intact. Light
from the open windows provided enough visibility to see the
dust floating in the air, waiting to land on the broken chairs,
tables, and the tavern bar of the once nice inn.

The inn was familiar, but due to the burnt interior and
scattered furniture, Jonathan couldn't place where he had seen
it before. He looked around and knew that it had once been
a tavern where travelers and local merchants participated in
festive meals and drinking. He could imagine the tavern with
roasting fires, clay lamps, and customers talking and laughing. But those days were gone, perhaps forever. Now there
was only enough light to make out broken furniture and the
remnants of a kitchen.

Jonathan made his way past the scattered chairs and tables to an open back door. There stood a pretty woman with slightly graying hair methodically preparing dinner. It was obvious she was once a beauty, but now age and hardship had made her simply a pretty woman, older but still graceful. Jonathan tried to smile.

She looked up and muttered, "What has Matthias dragged in now?" Stopping to take in Jonathan's disheveled hair, thread-bare garment, and hollow cheeks, she observed a simple truth. "You must be hungry."

Jonathan nodded affirmatively. He had not eaten since yesterday. He planned to bring his wages home, enough to purchase a chicken and vegetables for tomorrow's Sabbath meal. Without Matthias's rescue, the thieves would have undoubtedly caught him, stolen his wages, and then beaten him for the price of his resistance.

She nodded and continued with her meal preparations, offering a muted complaint. "Always bringing some lost soul to feed. For once he could think of feeding us first."

With those words, Matthias entered the room. "Yes, Susanna, have faith and our prayers will be answered. In the meantime, we are commanded to help those in need."

Susanna looked back at Matthias, with obvious pain in her eyes. She snapped back at him, "Where was our God when the Romans took over this land and made our lives no better than slaves?" Her voice strengthened and rose with her increasing anger. "Where is His promise to send us a new King, a Messiah to release us from this bondage? Where is our Moses?"

Susanna's voice broke as she continued, "Where is the mercy of your God? Go look toward Golgotha to see the crucifixions. And if you hadn't saved me, I'd still be a slave in Herod's palace! And why is it that the only ones profiting from this persecution are rabbis, Herod's tax collectors, and Romans?" Susanna was shaking when she rested her arm on the table.

Matthias quietly walked over and put his arms around Susanna.

She stopped her trembling and spoke softly to Matthias. "You have a good heart, my brother, but you cannot save everyone. Who is this boy?"

Jonathan sat quietly through Susanna's outburst. Then both Matthias and Susanna turned and faced Jonathan.

Matthias spoke first. "It's been a hard time for us all, Jonathan. Yes, I know who you are. Your father was a friend of mine—at least I always thought so. He was a good man. A long time ago we worked together."

"But . . ." Jonathan was clearly confused. His father was a carpenter. He was going to be his apprentice.

"As I was saying," interjected Matthias, "your dad and I were good friends. Then he met Sara, your mother, and his life changed. He realized he could no longer be the man he was. He desperately wanted to be a husband." Matthias paused. "And a father. I would occasionally see him working as a carpenter. The same attention to detail that made him a good partner served him well as a carpenter. But mostly, he was a good man because he had a passion to achieve something good. That passion was for you and your mother, Jonathan."

Jonathan gave Matthias a confused look.

"I miss his friendship and the man I could always trust with my life. But more honestly, I was jealous of his happiness, and his love for your mother." He paused, looking uncomfortable. "Jonathan, I was here when he died, in this very inn."

At that moment, Jonathan recognized where he was. The past years of pain, the struggle to stay alive, fell like a hammer striking an anvil. Jonathan staggered back toward the door, tripped on a stool, and fell.

Lying on the floor, he lost control, releasing his pain for the loss of a father who would never come home. Tears became shaking sobs. Jonathan's mouth gaped open as he unleashed years of loneliness, burdened to provide for his mother and sister. The agony he had buried deep just to survive, rolled over him as he lay on the floor, curled in on himself, trying to keep from breaking apart in grief and fear. He was incoherent and did not see Susanna kneel beside him. She held him by his shoulders.

Matthias continued after Susanna had calmed Jonathan. "This inn was burned the day after your father died."

Susanna sat down next to Jonathan, placed her hands on her cheeks, and quietly wept. She understood the pain this boy had suffered. So many in Jerusalem had met a similar fate. She gave Matthias a look he clearly understood. It was her turn to try to comfort Jonathan.

Susanna quietly placed her hands on Jonathan as his grief slowly subsided to the dull ache in his stomach that he had lived with since losing his father. Finally, she spoke. "I'm also aware that the Pharisees have walked away from helping your family. They believed your father to be a part of the resistance and would not compromise their position with the Romans and the prefect, so they stopped helping your mother. They knew it is written in the Torah to help you, but they dared not risk a rebellion. Just like the Magdalene family killed by the Romans six years ago. They set fire to the house and killed everyone except that young girl. No one lifted a finger to help her, poor girl."

Matthias couldn't contain himself any longer. "The Pharisees can be pigheaded. They may have kept the peace, but they lost the support of the Jews they serve. They are supposed to be here for us, and we are too cowardly to fight back. There are too many people suffering in Jerusalem, too much arrogance in the Temple, and too little help for those suffering and hungry."

Feeling awkward after his breakdown, Jonathan slowly got up and stared at Matthias. "What do you want from me?"

Jonathan waited for Matthias's answer. After a few minutes of contemplative silence, he spoke.

"I need an apprentice to help me as a tradesman. We find opportunities in the streets. There are always people needing something and others willing to sell it. We make the connections and fill the requirements for merchants and businesspeople in the city. But we must be first to make the deal, or someone else will make it before us." Matthias regarded the young man coolly. "And you need work to provide for your mother and your sister."

"Her name is Mara," Jonathan snapped.

"Well, do you want the work?"

Jonathan hesitated, staring back at Matthias "No! But I don't have any other offers and we need to survive."

Matthias walked over and looked Jonathan in the eyes. "Your father was an honorable man. I expect the same from you. You will keep two of every three coins you earn, and I'll take the third. That's the price for protecting, teaching, and feeding you."

Jonathan reached into his right palm and gave Matthias a coin with Caesar's face imprinted onto the roughly circular piece of copper. "This is yours. You saved me today and my mother will be grateful. I'll come back after the Sabbath."

At that, Jonathan turned and left. He had lost his appetite for trying to eat dinner in the same inn where he'd watched his father die years before. He needed to get home; his family needed the other two coins for food.

On the way home, Jonathan's head was swirling. He was caught between the pain of the past and an uncertain future. Jonathan felt alone. He didn't know where to go for advice, for help. Once again, he felt trapped.

Back in the inn, Matthias placed the coin in a clay jar hidden in the wall behind the door.

Susanna sat down and looked at Matthias, frowning and wrinkling her brow. "You still feel you owe Joseph for saving your life that night?"

It was hard for Matthias to respond or explain. Joseph had saved his life, throwing him against a wall just in time to avoid a Roman arrow aimed at his heart.

"That was a long time ago, Susanna. Some things are better forgotten." Matthias wished he could change the subject.

"But not for you, my brother. I know you." Susanna kept pressing Matthias. "You will never forget the debt you think you owe to a dead friend. I know you helped the boy's mother and sister after Joseph died."

"I could not let him or Sara go hungry. Everyone needs at least a small measure of hope." Matthias stared at Susanna, his tone becoming more defensive. "Many good men died that night. Do not bring up the subject again!" He stomped out of the building, walking away from dinner. He needed the night air to clear his mind and get some distance from the past he could not run away from.

Days later, as Jonathan made his way through the streets of Jerusalem to meet with Matthias, the sun was breaking free from its bonds of darkness, rising above the eastern walls of Jerusalem. At first, it was simply an eclipse, a hint of what was about to come. Slowly the sun transitioned into the brilliant golden-orange orb that dominated the eastern sky. Scattered red clouds crowned the brilliant sun, as though God accentuated the new day in Jerusalem.

Looking up at the rising sun and orange-red clouds, Jonathan paused. Perhaps this was the sign he desperately needed.

Entering the inn, he felt that his hesitation about his apprenticeship with Matthias had not diminished. But today there was also something new. A small measure of hope.

His father's death had not only upended his world, but it had accelerated him into manhood, hardening the edges of his youth. Jonathan had made a quiet vow to his father the night he died, promising to care for his mother and unborn sibling. He returned this morning with a renewed commitment to that vow.

Jonathan's promise became his new passion. Providing for them, caring for them, and most importantly, protecting his family drove Jonathan to become stronger, both physically and mentally.

'And to make money, lots of money. I want to be wealthy. Wealth would provide independence for my family,' he told himself.

First, he vowed to learn and become strong enough to be self-reliant. *'Never again will I have to beg for my family.'* He abhorred asking people for help and then watch them walk away in disdain. There was no room for weakness, no room for tears—just his passion to earn money.

"Matthias? Susanna?" Jonathan whispered as he entered the dilapidated inn. There was no response.

"Matthias?" he said louder, this time seeing a dim light, past the kitchen in the back of the inn. He slowly walked to the back room, avoiding the broken tables and chairs scattered around the inn's great room.

"You are early, Jonathan. Take some bread and cheese, you'll need it. It's going to be a full day," Matthias responded, putting on a tunic.

"Thanks," Jonathan said. "Why don't you clean up the place a bit, Matthias? It's difficult getting through the broken tables in the dark."

There was a moment of silence. Matthias was reluctant to explain, fearing it would bring bad memories for Jonathan. Finally, he decided to fill in the gaps.

"The inn has been abandoned since the fire; the clutter helps to keep people away. Children think it's haunted, and others stay away because they fear it brings bad luck."

Matthias thought it best to share some trust with Jonathan. "Jonathan, that is a secret only we share. I bought what was left of the inn after the fire burned most of it down. The previous owners just wanted to sell and get out of Jerusalem. I negotiated a good deal for the remains of the building and the land."

As Jonathan ate, Matthias continued, "It doesn't attract nosey Romans, tax collectors see no opportunities to collect here, and it keeps the curious away. It's the perfect place to stay inconspicuous."

Jonathan made a grunt of understanding between pieces of bread and goat cheese.

"Anyway, it's time to start your apprenticeship."

Jonathan watched as Matthias lit another clay lamp to brighten up the back room. "Did you have a chance to learn to read and write?"

Jonathan nodded and lifted his head as he replied. "Yes, I can read and write Aramaic. I can read and speak Hebrew, and I have some math instruction."

"Can you speak or write Latin or Greek? Have you had any history or political instruction?"

"No," responded Jonathan, looking down. "Though I have studied the Torah, so I know some history of the Jews."

"Fine. We can correct some of those shortcomings," Matthias said but didn't show any disappointment. He knew Jonathan had a good mind and was quick to act.

"Now, look around the room once and then tell me what you see," instructed Matthias.

Jonathan quickly turned around to glance at the room. He looked at Matthias and replied, "Two chairs, two tables, and a few jars."

"How many jars?" asked Matthias.

Jonathan hesitated and answered, "Five."

Matthias looked down and smiled. "Jonathan, not bad for a blind attempt. You missed four jars and the chair in the corner, also, what was on the table and the types of jars in the room." Matthias explained, "What we do is exchange opportunities for profit. The first thing we need to teach you is to observe and recognize opportunities. Jerusalem is full of people who need things to survive. They need food, clothes, shelter, protection, and the means to make a living. You know this intuitively. Then there are those who want more, want to make money and buy things. They understand what they want, but not always how they can get what they want."

"I understand." Jonathan started to relax and let down a few of his fear barriers.

Matthias explained the point of the day's drill. "To make money, we need to understand the customer's needs before they do, and certainly before other traders do. We need to see opportunities that exist and opportunities that will appear in the future. So, the first thing you need to learn is to open your eyes."

Jonathan nodded his understanding.

"We'll begin and end each day with these drills, and some additional education. I need you to open your eyes, see everything you can, and then start to anticipate events before they happen. In this way, you can position us to have the right merchandise to sell to those who wake up and realize they need to buy what we have. Now, tell me what else is happening in Jerusalem."

For two hours Jonathan was grilled by Matthias on his views of life in Jerusalem. As Jonathan systematically answered his questions, he realized that his views of Jerusalem had been heavily influenced by his drive to earn quick money. By the end of the day, having completed numerous chores assigned by Matthias, Jonathan was exhausted and went home with his head spinning.

MATTHIAS

What Matthias learned that morning was that Jonathan had gifts, the ability to understand political and social relationships, and a quick and accurate mathematical mind.

"Susanna, he's got some talent." But what Matthias was really searching for was another opinion from his sister. Despite her anger toward what was happening in Jerusalem, Matthias trusted her insights and instincts.

"Yes, and he is driven. His passion will ensure he works hard to succeed," she responded. "But he also has an edge of mistrust and hardness that comes from tragedy and growing up too fast. Try to help him not let his bitterness overtake his soul."

Matthias knew she could see things in others that even he missed. For this reason, he respected her opinion and pondered how he would alter Jonathan's training to keep those dark forces from his life. He wondered if he could.

THE JOURNEYMAN

For several months, Matthias balanced Jonathan's training with physical labor, for which he paid Jonathan 2/3
of a journeyman's salary. Most tasks consisted of cleaning
or moving goods to be delivered or picking up purchased
stores for future resale. As Jonathan completed each task, he
was given the responsibility to ensure the right amount of
goods were purchased or delivered and that he transported
the items to the right person or place, getting signatures for
delivery or pickup.

After six months of drills and menial tasks, Matthias
asked two friends to test Jonathan's skills, temperament, and
honesty. The first merchant was Joshua, a friend who had
known Matthias for over fifteen years and owed him many
favors. Joshua intentionally shortchanged Jonathan by providing less wheat than was paid for. Jonathan paid full price
without weighing the wheat and left for the warehouse as
Matthias had instructed.

After arriving at the warehouse, Jonathan used the scales
to recheck the weight of the wheat, discovering it was short.
At first, he was afraid that Matthias would accuse him of
cheating, then realized his only course of action was to face
the merchant with the wheat and apparent shortage.

"Sir, the wheat you sold me was short by five librae. As
Moses is my witness, I am not lying to you," Jonathan stated,
trying his best not to accuse Joshua of cheating him.

At first, the merchant denied the shortage, as Matthias
had instructed. But Jonathan continued to press the issue.
Settling his voice and continuing to press Joshua, Jonathan

looked Joshua in the eye. "Sir, you are a faithful trader with Matthias, for whom I am a trusted agent. We have plans to expand our trade and count on you to become a central part of that expansion. We need your trust and fair dealings."

After continuing his arguments, finally Jonathan won his case, and the merchant reweighed the wheat and provided additional wheat. Jonathan returned to the warehouse with the appropriate wheat, not mentioning the episode to Matthias.

Matthias's second test of Jonathan was with Ben, a man Matthias trusted and had befriended in childhood. Matthias sent Jonathan to buy twenty bushels of corn for the Roman garrison in Fort Antonia. When Jonathan arrived, he found the corn already in grain sacks, tied and stacked onto a cart.

At first, Jonathan looked carefully at the sacks and then decided to untie a bushel near the bottom of the cart. What he found was a mixture of corn and straw in the sacks. Jonathan immediately refused the corn and asked to talk to Ben privately.

"Sir, I am young but no fool. If you try to sell us straw again it will be known throughout Jerusalem that you are a dishonest merchant." Jonathan then walked away.

Jonathan returned to Matthias and explained that the merchant didn't have the corn ready and that he would need to deliver the corn to Herod's palace in Jerusalem the following day. The following morning Jonathan inspected the corn, then paid Ben, looking him directly in the eyes. He quickly delivered the corn to Herod's palace, as instructed, and refunded a few shekels to Chusa, the kitchen master, for delivering the corn late.

Jonathan returned to the inn, paid Matthias, and explained the discount shortage he had given the Roman quartermaster. He told Matthias he would make up the difference from his coins, and then went home. Jonathan had said nothing about the merchant trying to cheat them.

After Jonathan had gone, Matthias turned to Susanna. "He's good, Susanna—the kid is good."

"What did you tell him when he told you Ben had tried to cheat him?" asked Susanna.

"That's the amazing thing, he never told me about Joshua and Ben trying to cheat him. He just handled it and never said a word," replied Matthias. "I talked to them both. They said he never got angry, just warned them that while he was young, he was not stupid, and he was going to be around for a long time. He told them we were expanding, and he wanted to do business with them in the future but needed to be able to trust them, otherwise, they would gain a reputation as unworthy merchants."

Matthias continued, "I see a lot of Joseph in him, standing up for himself and not backing down when cheated. But unlike Joseph, he keeps his head and doesn't overreact. He understands that mutual trust will build future opportunities."

"I told you he was smart," Susanna smiled.

For the next few months, Matthias watched Jonathan closely, sometimes following him and talking to trusted friends to see how Jonathan handled himself. He needed verification that his view of Jonathan was the same as others. He was not disappointed and as the months became a year, Jonathan had Matthias's complete trust and confidence.

JONATHAN

Working for Matthias, Jonathan started to see a steady income. He was making enough money for his family to survive without fear of starvation or homelessness. For the first time since his father had died, Jonathan and his family had some stability.

It was after the first year that Jonathan's lessons transitioned into learning Greek and sharpening his math skills. In addition, Matthias added discussions about politics and how the changing nature of Jerusalem would bring business opportunities. Jonathan was no longer just working to deliver merchandise that Matthias had previously bought or sold. Matthias was allowing Jonathan to find opportunities for himself. With Matthias's help, he began making trades. Jonathan learned to listen and ask questions. What he found, to his amazement, was that people wanted to talk about their businesses and their lives.

Jonathan started to learn that he had to be trusted to be respectable and to be trusted he had to listen and remember what was important to others, particularly his future customers. He started to understand he didn't always know when he was talking to a future client, so he humbled himself and faded into someone who lived in the background of Jerusalem society. He was there but unseen. Because he was young and openly respectful, he gained the trust of the people around him. Because he would not be cheated and was strong-willed, he also gained their respect. He was becoming more and more like his mentor and growing friend, Matthias.

On a quiet morning in June, Matthias approached Jonathan while he was eating breakfast in the burnt inn.

"I'm worried about the Jewish resistance, Jonathan. It's growing. The people are starting to support the Zealot rebellion and it's bad for business. If it continues, the Romans will strike hard, and we Jews will pay the price for their undisciplined revolt. Life is hard enough. It will be harder for everyone. The Pharisees will not be able to negotiate with the prefect to stop Roman retaliations, and Golgotha will be full of crucifixions."

"The garrison at Fortress Antonia will grow as well," Jonathan replied.

"Maybe the Romans will finally get a small measure of the cruelty they give us without a second thought," interjected Susanna.

Both Matthias and Jonathan flinched. But it was Matthias who raised his voice. "And the bloodshed will flow throughout Judea! Is that what you want?"

"No, you know that. But justice must come someday. Someday the Messiah will come," Susanna quietly said, knowing the subject to be sensitive to both her brother and Jonathan.

"Anyway, Jonathan, be careful and on the lookout for trouble," Matthias finished.

Chapter 6

PRAYERS

24 AD

JERUSALEM

The stone wall of the garden was cool and refreshing from the heat of the day. Jonathan lay back and stared at the stars and his favorite constellation, Leo, the Lion of Judah. At two in the morning, the Garden of Gethsemane was empty, except for Jonathan and a wandering sheep that had strayed from a nearby pasture.

"Lord, I haven't talked to You since Father died. I miss him so much. I was so angry with you, Lord. You took him seven years ago. We still don't understand. Whose sin are we paying for? Are you still angry with us?"

As he spoke, the wind whistled through the garden, providing a harmonic tone to Jonathan's sorrow. The sheep paused and bayed at Jonathan. A starling passed overhead and landed in a nearby olive tree. Jonathan sat quietly as the starling sang his evening song.

"Is this a sign you have forgiven me, Lord? How deep, how wide is Your love? Like the Jordan, is Your love forever there, forever flowing? Will You keep me in Your heart?"

Jonathan silently cried in frustration and loneliness. In the darkness of the early morning, the garden was his only sanctuary where he could give voice to his fears.

"I'm scared, Lord. My family thinks I'm smart, but how can I be smart if we've lost everything? I just work harder now. You know the truth about me: I'm a fraud." Jonathan paused and then let out his shame.

"Lord, you can be angry with me, but I feel ashamed that I couldn't stop the soldiers. I was afraid. They were too big for me. I couldn't stop my father from dying. I tried."

Jonathan swallowed and continued, "Lord, punish me, but please have mercy on my mother and Mara. They worship you so much and yet they are in such pain. Help them, Lord, and protect them in your heart. But Lord, I'm still afraid, ashamed."

Jonathan wiped tears from his cheeks as the starling continued his evening song. The lone sheep slowly stepped closer to Jonathan, disappointed in the lack of grass in the garden. Lying on the stone wall, Jonathan soon fell asleep, curled between the stones and the sheep who had laid down next to him. The starling continued his song, eventually joined by another.

Jonathan slept peacefully, free from the haunting nightmares that had plagued him. He had found a small measure of peace in Gethsemane.

Before dawn, Jonathan rose to the screech of an owl. He gathered his belongings that had become wet from the morning dew and rushed home to let his mother know he was ok and heading to work.

Matthias had already warned Jonathan it would be a hard day for both of them. There was a special delivery of wheat that would take them the majority of the day to pick up and deliver. After a quick breakfast, Matthias rushed Jonathan out the door, walking quickly in the cool of the morning. It would be another hot day in Jerusalem and the hard labor had to be done before noon.

When he arrived at a stone warehouse, Jonathan nodded to Matthias, who had ordered him to begin hitching up donkeys to the twelve carts loaded with wheat. Within the hour they were making their way through Jerusalem, the steady noise of the donkeys' hooves echoing through the empty streets.

"Jonathan, keep the carts moving, we need to move quickly."

Jonathan nodded. As they progressed through Jerusalem, it became clear their destination was Fortress Antonia. These bushels of wheat were meant for Roman soldiers. He shuddered at the thought of feeding those heathens, the same soldiers who kept his people in bondage, crucified anyone who opposed their will, and killed his father.

Matthias stopped, turned to Jonathan, and gave him a stern look. "You must take opportunities where you get them, Jonathan. You'll need to remember this."

Jonathan nodded and lowered his head to hide his face in the hood of his cloak. Inside, he bristled. He knew Matthias was right. The important thing was to survive, to prosper in preparation for the day when they could fight for their freedom.

Jonathan drove the donkeys harder through the city's streets.

An hour later, they entered the gates of the fortress, directed by the guards to the legion quartermaster. It was another hour before the Roman quartermaster finally came down after his morning duties. After twenty minutes of Matthias haggling over the price, Jonathan watched as the quartermaster finally nodded his head and instructed his squadron of soldiers to unload the carts.

"Don't just stand there looking at the wheat, get these carts unloaded into the storeroom!" another officer shouted to his men. "We have weapon drills this morning and we can't be delayed moving supplies. Move!"

Jonathan looked up and thought there was something familiar about the young Roman officer shouting orders. Shaking his head at the knot in his stomach, he kept his distance until it was time to gather the donkeys for the return trip. Jonathan wanted to leave that place, the sooner the better.

After another two hours in the August morning heat, Jonathan and Matthias arrived at the warehouse and unhitched the empty carts.

"We'll need to wash and feed the donkeys," said Matthias. "It's been a hot morning for us all, especially the donkeys. Ensure they get enough water."

Jonathan nodded and started to clean the donkeys and draw water from a local cistern. By the time Matthias and Jonathan returned to the inn, it was midafternoon. Both were tired, sweaty, and hungry as they entered the inn and saw Susanna preparing a late lunch for the two. For the first time that day, Jonathan broke out into a hard-earned smile.

The next day they delivered another load to the Roman Fort, two dozen bushels of onions and two barrels of olive oil. Jonathan knew Matthias was working hard to establish an inroad into the Jerusalem food supplies market, despite their distaste for selling to the Roman soldiers. Rumors abounded throughout Jerusalem that Rome was adding more soldiers to Fortress Antonia, to get the legion's strength up to the normal 6,000 soldiers and 4,000 support troops. If Matthias and Jonathan could deliver a steady source of wheat, barley, oil, and corn, they would make good and steady profits. They just needed to keep the trust of the Romans.

As Jonathan walked back to the inn, he turned and saw Matthias smile.

"You worked hard today. I know working with the Romans is difficult for you. It's hard for me, too. But it's important, Jon."

Jonathan muttered, "I understand."

"Your eyes tell me you don't understand," Matthias shot back. "Some things we must do, things we detest to get a greater reward. Feeding those heathens will help us prosper. If we can gain wealth, then we open our future. Your family will be safer."

Jonathan looked up and nodded to Matthias, this time looking directly into his eyes. Jonathan saw the truth of Matthias's words, yet he still detested the Romans and wanted revenge.

"Someday. Someday there will be . . ." he whispered.

"Yes, Jon, someday there will be justice," Matthias finished his thought.

They arrived back at the inn as Susanna was preparing another late afternoon meal. Entering the back rooms, they both collapsed onto benches against the wall.

"Jon, you haven't talked much about Sara and Mara. How are they?" asked Matthias to remove thoughts of today's efforts from Jonathan's mind.

"They are well. Thanks to you, we were able to survive for those three years before I started to work for you," Jonathan replied.

Matthias was taken aback. Susanna stopped her meal preparations to look at Jonathan.

"I thought the streets could keep at least some secrets. But it was a debt to your father that I was repaying. Nothing more."

"You mean the night Father pulled you away from a Roman lance during your defense of the Magdala?"

Stunned, Matthias turned and looked at Jonathan. He was becoming a seasoned businessman, pulling disparate pieces of information together to fill in the gaps in his personal history. He was no longer a student, but not yet a master.

"Yes, and several other occasions as well. In my youth, I was stronger than I was smart. And those secrets are better left forgotten. The streets have ears and there's always a price for information that would tease the Romans."

"Matthias, you've paid your debt to my father many times over. Not to mention saving me in the alley that first day. And I am grateful for your teachings and employment. I will always be in both of your debts." Jonathan finished his meal and again looked Matthias in the eyes. "Thank you. God bless you for your kindness."

Matthias laughed. "Don't thank me yet. Tomorrow we are moving two dozen bushels of apples, two barrels of olive oil, and forty bushels of corn. You'll need your rest. There are still many days of hard labor ahead."

Jonathan finished his meal and started to leave the inn. He turned and asked, "Matthias, what do you think this inn is worth?" Then before Matthias could answer, he turned and walked out the door.

Matthias's smile turned into a grimace. Jonathan was changing so quickly; he was learning faster than Matthias had expected and he was worried. He could see the hardness that Susanna had identified growing in Jonathan. He could only pray that he was helping Jonathan and Sara, not creating something he would regret later.

In many ways, the boy was becoming more calculating, except when dealing with his mother and sister. Matthias had hoped that the money he earned would be the leverage he needed to rise above the tragedy of the past.

As he walked home, Jonathan looked down at his hand. He could count success in his palm. It was shiny, it was real, and it could be saved for a day of need. If he could only keep this reflection of his worth in a hidden place, safe from the Romans, Pharisees, and tax collectors.

But Jonathan's passion to earn money for his family wasn't enough. It was also a means to prove his life had worth. But as with all his successes, there was always a price to be paid.

CASSIUS

"Don't let them cheat you again, Cephas!" shouted Cassius as he sized up his new replacement guard. "The last batch of onions coming out of Samaria was a full measure short, you blockhead! Watch these new merchants carefully."

Cephas winced as he headed toward the gate to receive supplies for the quartermaster. His new supervisor had already come with a stern reputation, and Cephas wasn't prepared to suffer the consequences of trusting out-of-town merchants again without weighing supply deliveries carefully.

Across the courtyard, Tribune Valens watched Cassius direct the daily food supplies into the storerooms. While this task was normally assigned to the legion quartermaster, Tribune Valens wanted to test Cassius's operational leadership skills. As the newest Roman Standard, it was clear Cassius could fight, but Valens needed his young officer to learn every aspect of the Roman army. Without logistics, the Army was a day's meal away from defeat.

"How do you find your new duties, Cassius?"

In truth, Cassius saw the daily grind of supervising replacements, establishing watch schedules, monitoring guards, and overseeing supplies as pure drudgery. He hadn't expected these duties with his recent promotion. Yet despite his distaste for bureaucracy, he never voiced a complaint.

Cassius saluted. "Demanding but manageable, sir."

"Nicely put, Cassius. The administration of the encamped legion can overwhelm most officers. I hear you are doing well."

"Sir? I'm doing my best and learning," replied Cassius.

Valens laughed. "Keep up your efforts. You won't be a quartermaster officer for long."

Cassius smiled as his favorite officer walked away. Ever since he learned about Tribune Valens being a friend of his father, he held a fondness for the Tribune. Especially since his father risked his life to save this man. *'Someday I'll be able to repay my debt to Bracus . . . perhaps someday I can save someone worthy from certain death,'* Cassius vowed to himself.

Command and combat had given Cassius the direct demeanor of leadership. Still keeping to himself even eight years after Bracus's death, Cassius used his spare time for combat drills, exercising, and finding books in Herod's library. In the eyes of the legion leadership, Cassius had become the perfect Roman soldier.

Yet Cassius also held secrets. His passion for learning had not wavered since his youth. Sightings of Cassius near Herod's library brought questions, despite his discretion, but he continued to find solace there. Few suspected he was in Herod's palace to read about history, politics, and mathematics in Greek and Aramaic.

His other passion had become exercising the fortress stable horses. With a mix of Arabian and European stallions, geldings, and mares, Cassius found a perfect variety to challenge his riding skills. His favorite was Venti, Prefect Ambivulus's well-known Andalusian that Marcus Ambivulus, now a Senator, had left as a gift to the Roman Xth Legion, specifically in the care of Cassius. Few riders other than Cassius would dare ride the powerful Andalusian.

After giving instructions to his sergeant to complete the offloading of food supplies, Cassius walked through

Jerusalem to check on his guards in Herod's palace. Satisfied his men were properly stationed, Cassius decided to return to the fortress stables.

Cassius gazed at the long rows of over two hundred horses in open stables. The aroma of horse flesh, manure, and people working to clean the stalls overwhelmed most visitors. But none of the sights and smells bothered Cassius—he had grown up with these smells. The whinnying of horses before their grain reminded him of home. Cassius watched as Ethiopian and Egyptian servants desperately tried to keep up the cleaning, grooming, and feeding of the 200 horses in the stable. Carts of horse manure waited to be hauled outside of Fortress Antonia while men dragged buckets of water to the horse stalls. Flies were everywhere.

As Cassius walked down the long aisles of conscripts, the men stopped working until he passed by, waiting to see if the Roman officer had orders for them. After about five minutes of walking through the stables, Cassius spotted his favorite horse, the black Andalusian.

Approaching Venti, Cassius took a brush and started long, angular strokes across Venti's black torso and massive neck. Grooming Venti reminded Cassius of his youth, how his father had insisted on an immaculately groomed horse before the boys could ride.

But today Cassius had apprehensions. It was the first time he would take Venti outside Jerusalem, into the open spaces of Judea. Could he maintain control of this raging tornado? In the end, it was his pride that drove him to mount the shining black equine.

Five minutes later, Cassius entered the streets of Jerusalem, and Venti began to test him. At first, Venti just pranced, lifting his legs high to let Cassius know he was ready to run. Then suddenly Venti erupted in the streets, spinning around and around, expressing his power and grace. After knocking over a table of figs and olives, Cassius held Venti with both reins, mustering all his strength to control the beast, and Venti responded by gripping the reins tightly between his teeth.

Merchants stopped to see the young Roman officer, riding a magnificent, shining black Andalusian as though they were both statues. After five minutes of willful struggle, Cassius's muscles started to bulge and cramp from the ordeal. Finally, he maintained enough control to guide Venti past the north gate of Jerusalem, onto the north road toward Samaria.

As soon as they had passed the crowded entrance of the city, Cassius eased control of Venti's reins, allowing him to lower his head, stretch his front legs, and burst into a run. Venti was galloping within seconds. Cassius balanced himself as Venti pushed forward, faster. Venti increased his gallop with another burst of energy, throwing Cassius slightly backward. Both horse and rider were just short of uncontrollable speed.

Cassius chuckled as he realized Venti had been locked up in the stables for too long. Soon the morning haze and wind began to sting Cassius's eyes. Yet neither Cassius nor Venti showed any signs of wanting to slow down.

As Cassius continued along the road to Bethel, he saw dust rise from a group of horsemen riding across the apex of a hill and onto the open chaparral from the east. They rode directly towards him. As they came closer, Cassius realized these men were armed, carrying bows and lances.

They rode in close formation, but these riders were not Romans, not bandits; they were armed Zealots. After the first set of arrows flew in his direction, Cassius understood these trained archers could aim and launch arrows while riding galloping horses. Cassius looked down at his only defense, his gladius sword. It was too short of a sword to protect against the bows and lances of the oncoming soldiers. As the Zealots closed in on Cassius, they launched another set of four arrows that missed Venti by a foot, landing in the dirt behind Cassius.

Cassius squeezed Venti's chest with his legs, pushing him forward with his hips, and pulled his reigns to the right. Venti responded by locking his hindquarters, sliding to a stop, and spinning around on his haunches. The horse jumped to a full gallop, back toward Jerusalem.

Cassius continued to push Venti hard, creating a longer lead ahead of the approaching Zealots. Another five minutes and Cassius and Venti were beyond arrow range, quickly increasing the distance from their pursuers. Dust pounded Cassius in the face, his eyes blurring as tears tried to keep dirt from obscuring his vision. Determined to escape, Cassius continued to push Venti hard to further extend his lead.

As Cassius glanced behind to check the distance of the Zealots, he realized that twenty minutes of galloping had exhausted their horses, which had slowed to a walk, breathing heavily. Eventually, they reined in their horses to turn around and give up the chase. Cassius smiled and relaxed his legs, giving Venti the signal to slow to a canter.

He could smell Venti's sweat, a foam lather that covered the horse's chest and neck, along with the sweat-soaked leather of the saddle and reins. The sight of the road and the smells of Venti froze Cassius in a different time, a different place.

Riding through the wheat fields, Cassius looked over to see Bracus, riding shoulder to shoulder atop horses at a gallop. Bracus was laughing at the top of his lungs, arms spread like an eagle trying to fly. It was only during these times that Cassius and Bracus found their true freedom, riding across the plains of Tuscany. Cassius would always keep his horse between the thin line of a controlled gallop and running with abandon.

Cassius awoke from the moment to find himself alone with Venti.

After ten minutes of cantering, both horse and rider were approaching fatigue. Cassius and Venti seemed to agree, it was time to slow to a trot, then walk. Walking was easy. Cassius matched Venti's rhythmic sway with his hips. Letting his sandals fall out of the stirrups, Cassius stretched his legs. They moved as one, horse and rider.

As they approached Jerusalem, Venti saw the city. Lifting his head, the horse sniffed the familiar air of Jerusalem and broke into a trot.

"Don't worry, Venti. They all know you're a stallion." Cassius laughed and patted Venti's thick black neck. He watched his magnificent horse flex his shoulders, light reflecting off the curvature of his muscles.

"Have the gods given me this magnificent horse to appease my loneliness?" Cassius thought aloud. "Are you as alone as I am, Venti?"

In Jerusalem, Cassius dismounted. They walked through the streets, and Cassius no longer felt as alone in Judea as he had before the ride. For the first time, Cassius saw Venti as a trusted friend. Venti snorted in response.

"You are free to be a horse, Venti. Whether tamed or wild, you are a beautiful horse. I no longer understand who I am, or whom I am becoming. I just ride the storm. Thank you for being there with me," he whispered.

Venti turned to look at him and snorted in agreement.

As they walked to Fortress Antonia and back to their lives of service and confinement, Cassius was caught in a moment of another fantasy. Freedom could be purchased with a fast gallop and a life outside of his past—no more legion responsibilities or living up to his Roman masters.

'Could I run away from my past? No more killing?' he asked himself.

He whispered to Venti, "No matter where I am, I will always have masters. Yet freedom is just a gallop away for you."

Despite his reluctance, he led Venti back to the stables, their bonds of servitude re-established. The fleeting attraction of freedom was not strong enough to overcome their trained responsibilities.

Back in the stables, he fed Venti fresh hay, burying his face deep into his mane. "Someday, Venti, we will be free to run."

As Cassius walked out of the stables, he turned to find Venti staring at him from over his barrier. The horse whinnied as though asking Cassius why he was leaving. Cassius hesitated, then forced himself to walk out of the stables.

Passing the southern gate of Fortress Antonia and back into the streets of Jerusalem, Cassius's thoughts of being chased by Zealots turned to anger. He was exhausted, covered in dust, and soaked in his and Venti's sweat. Yet his mind was still racing from a lingering adrenalin rush.

Arriving back in Fortress Antonia, Cassius walked directly to the quarters of his centurion, Clavius Orestes, who was speaking to Tribune Valens.

"Will these Hebrews ever give up? They are conquered!" Startled at Cassius's entrance, the centurion stared at the sight of him, covered with dust and sweat.

"Is it your custom to interrupt your senior officers, Cassius?" asked Tribune Valens.

Cassius quickly saluted. "My apologies, Tribune. I was unaware you were here."

"Continue, Cassius, now that you have interrupted our conversation. We were just discussing the Hebrews. What news do you bring?" Centurion Orestes shot a commanding stare at Cassius.

"I was attacked on the north road, sir. There were a dozen mounted Zealots, armed with javelins and bows. Fortunately, their aim was worse than their ability to ride, but they did chase me back several miles to Jerusalem. They were looking to kill me and steal my horse, not for bounty or ransom."

Centurion Orestes looked at Tribune Valens with a grimace.

"The rebels are becoming more brazen, attacking a Roman officer just outside of Jerusalem!" Cassius continued.

Tribune Valens turned to look at his centurion and waited for a reaction.

Orestes's reply was quick and cruel: "You know they only understand drastic measures. We have tried everything else!"

Cassius lowered his head, realizing he would inevitably be a part of those drastic measures, often aimed at Jews who never participated in the attacks. It was a task he did not covet or condone. A nagging fear was growing inside Cassius—he was becoming too accustomed to death. After leading two dozen skirmishes with Zealot rebels in and outside the city, rarely would an ambush or raid end without at least several Romans or Zealots dead.

"It is a price that must be paid for keeping the peace in this forsaken land," said Cassius. Valens quietly nodded but said nothing.

"Orestes, I'll talk to Prefect Pontius Pilate about this incident. He's new to Jerusalem. But he wants to keep the peace through a balance, not brute force," explained Valens. "In the meantime, I'll order an increase in patrols within the city and outside the neighboring area. Perhaps we can get lucky and find spies that are more interested in money than integrity. In the meantime, Cassius, get cleaned up and go brief King Herod. He'll need this information as well." Valens dismissed Cassius.

Cassius, frustrated, returned to his quarters for a long-awaited bath. Rubbing down his calluses and sore muscles in hot water, he was grateful for the small relief. He thought of Venti and his ride to freedom. Pondering the upcoming Roman retaliation, his anger and frustration rose. He felt no lust for more killing.

Cassius dressed quickly, anxious to give King Herod a quick brief so he could return to the fortress stables. He wanted to give Venti a good wash and ensure he had extra hay and grain for the night.

Walking up to his sergeant of the guards, Cassius announced, "Sergeant, inform the guards for Herod's palace I'll be walking over to the palace with them. We leave in 15 minutes. I understand we are early, but I need to see Herod right away."

As Cassius and his guards marched through the streets of Jerusalem, the smells of evening meal preparations stung against his stomach. His hunger was well deserved, as his last meal had been a pre-dawn slice of bread and cheese. The sight of boiling vegetables, baking bread, and roasted rabbits only increased his frustration and temper.

Entering the palace, Cassius issued the guards instructions for the evening and ordered the relieved guards back to the fortress. Across the open courtyard, Cassius climbed the stairs to the second level of King Herod's quarters. He ordered the stationed guard to announce his presence. After ten minutes of waiting, the guard returned and escorted Cassius to King Herod.

Herod sat at his dining table, perched three feet above the main hall. "What information do you have, Standard?" he asked before Cassius could provide the required salutary formalities.

Cassius saluted and knelt. "Sire, I was riding just outside of Jerusalem this afternoon when I came across a group of twelve Jewish rebels. I find this unusual for two reasons. First, they were operating just three miles from Jerusalem's gates, and second, they brazenly attacked a Roman officer," replied Cassius. "Your Highness, it appears to me they are increasing in strength and aggressiveness."

Herod raised his head and looked down upon Cassius. "What? Are you a general, to consult me on the meaning of such activities? Is one incident a mass rebellion against my authority?"

"No sire, my apologies. Please forgive my personal views." Cassius's anger grew at the arrogance of Herod. "Tribune Valens was aware of the significance of the growing rebel attacks and thought you might take a different political point of view on today's incidents."

"Go back to your guard duties, Cassius. If you are that concerned, then ensure your guards take extra caution to protect me against these rumors!" Herod turned to his meal with his new bride Herodias and her daughter Salome.

"As you command." Cassius saluted and backed out of Herod's quarters. He grimaced at Herod's arrogance as he turned and headed toward the palace courtyard.

Cassius felt as though his stomach was going to punch a hole in his abdomen. He needed food and a place to calm down from the Zealots' attack and King Herod's insults. He changed his direction and marched toward the palace kitchens. Bursting past the kitchen door, Cassius yelled for a meal. "I am starving. What do you have to eat?"

KITCHEN MAID

As Cassius pushed the kitchen door open, the young maid who was leaving with fruit and wine, stumbled backward in surprise. Mary screamed, spilling half the wine as the fruit scattered across the floor. Looking down in horror, she knew she would be punished for her failure to protect the King's food.

Mary looked up at Cassius and held back her anger as she put the wine jug on a table and started to collect the fruit.

Taken aback, Cassius realized his anger had caused the crash. He had taken his anger out on an innocent servant; he knew he was being rude. He jumped toward the servant girl to help reclaim the fruit. The sudden move from a tall Roman officer further frightened Mary and she flinched from his approach, backing up to the kitchen wall. Cassius felt even worse.

"My apologies, maid, I did not mean to frighten you." As Cassius spoke, he picked up fruit and carried it to the wash basin for cleaning. He looked up and saw the frightened young woman with tears flowing down her reddened face. She shivered when he approached. Her headdress had fallen, revealing her deep black hair that flowed past her shoulders.

Cassius made a quick decision to resolve the situation. "I will accompany you to the king's table to ensure you are not harmed because of my rudeness."

Mary looked up at Cassius with angry eyes, but her tears betrayed her fears.

Cassius looked directly into her eyes. What he found was something he had never expected. He stepped back, stunned.

In front of Cassius was a young servant woman with black hair, hazel eyes, and a bronze complexion. She was simply beautiful. Her garments could not hide her figure. He blushed in embarrassment. Her beauty left a mark on his mind. He realized why she had been chosen to serve King Herod.

"Thank you, centurion." Mary barely spoke above a whisper, her lips stretched in anger. "I am sorry, but I am a servant in this palace. I do not want to be beaten again."

Cassius hesitated, realizing he was making the situation worse. "I am only a standard; my superior is Centurion Orestes. My name is Cassius." Cassius stumbled for something intelligent to say. "As I said, I will accompany you to the king's quarters to ensure no fault is brought upon you." Cassius tried an awkward smile and he saw her relax slightly. He could see she was unsure of his intentions.

"If you are ready, I'm going now to see King Herod and will accompany you," Cassius lied.

He held the door as they left with a new wine jug and clean fruit.

Walking slowly through the courtyard and up to Herod's quarters, Cassius looked down on Mary, who kept her gaze straight forward. Passing the Roman guard into Herod's dining chamber, Cassius gave his soldier a dangerous glare, his eyes clearly telling the guard, *'Mind your business and open the blasted door!'*

By the time Mary had arrived with additional fruit for the evening meal, King Herod and his guests had already consumed enough food and wine to be fully reclined on their cushions, drunk enough to be relaxed and jovial. Cassius was not surprised that no one at the table had noticed when Mary delivered the food. She turned and backed away quickly to avoid attention. Cassius walked out with Mary.

Suddenly King Herod shouted, laughing as he spoke. "Cassius! Are you now protecting my food deliveries? Has the rebel's attack frightened you this much?"

"Sire, my duties are only for your safety," responded Cassius as he backed out of the king's chambers.

As they returned to the kitchen, neither one spoke a word, not wanting to break the awkward silence between them. Cassius was not accustomed to talking to women, especially one who had slapped him into humility with her beauty.

When they entered the kitchen, Mary said without looking at Cassius, "You said you were starving. We have leftover chicken, some figs, blackberries, and dates. I'm sorry but the bread is gone for today, and the baker won't arrive for another four hours."

"You are my savior, young maid," Cassius blurted. "I certainly would not have survived the night without food." Cassius immediately regretted his awkward words. Trying to cover his nervousness, he smiled awkwardly and felt even more stupid.

Without looking back at him, Mary released a sigh of relief, smiled to herself, and prepared the meal. After setting out the food for Cassius, she left quickly without a word to him.

Cassius was confused by this woman, and it frustrated him. He chose the only escape he knew. After quickly finishing the meal, he walked across the courtyard again and into a lesser-known room in the palace: the library.

Cassius sometimes managed to steal a few hours to himself, and his destination was always the same. In the corners of King Herod's library, he could escape between the stacks of scrolls and books. There were worlds he could retreat into without risking his life. Captured in these moments of solitude, he felt as though the realities of his life were less harsh. There was no other thought but for the words on the page.

But tonight, he struggled to maintain his focus. The young kitchen maid had settled deeply into his consciousness. His mind had been caught in a trap he could not escape.

MARY

"So, you met the new Standard of the Guard?" Joanna smiled at Mary.

"Stop that, Joanna. He's clumsy and stiff-necked. And he's a Roman!"

"You can't hide your beauty from everyone, Mary. He's handsome—for a Roman, I mean."

"Joanna don't ever forget we are bonded slaves. They call us servants, but we are slaves. Just try to leave. How many lashes did Leah get when she left the palace to secretly meet with Aphra?" Mary walked out of the small room they shared next to the storerooms.

In the corridor outside the kitchens, Mary cried in frustration. She'd tried desperately to make herself invisible to both Herod's guards and the Romans. And despite her long black hair, smooth skin, and striking features, the only reason Mary was left alone was her seizures. Many in the palace believed she was possessed by demons. Mary used her infrequent seizures to remain separate, while still working hard to show she could be trusted by the palace manager, Chuza, and his staff.

Yet Mary was still afraid of Roman soldiers, the same soldiers who had killed her parents. Now she was angry at herself for even thinking about the clumsy Roman officer, fueled by the fact she could find no malice or arrogance in Cassius. This was not what she had expected, and it unsettled her. For a moment she thought she had seen the same dark pain in Cassius that she carried.

Coming around the corner, Chuza looked up and was surprised to see Mary coming toward him and crying.

"Please leave me alone!" she sobbed before he could say anything. She ran into the storerooms. Chuza frowned and continued down the hall to Mary and Joanna's room.

"Joanna, is there a problem?"

Chapter 7

THE PRICE OF LUMBER

26 AD

JERUSALEM

MATTHIAS

The sun was setting in Jerusalem and the long western shadows of the city were fading in the late fall months.

At the end of the vacant fruit market, an alley between two warehouses led to the neighborhood meat market. Customers passing through the alley didn't give a second look at the old man begging for money. They just walked by and pretended not to notice. Some even quickened their pace past the alley to avoid the beggar's attention.

The beggar was a stout man and didn't seem to be unduly harmed by his miserable situation. Yet his garments were torn by years of wear and river washing. His burlap tunic was shredded at the hem, hanging just above his knees. His black kufiyah headdress covered his head and shoulders, but his beard was clearly visible. The intensity of the beggar's eyes marked him as a desperate man, in need of selling the pitiful cloth scraps he held out to passersby, which might ensure a meager meal. The beggar's hand motions were exaggerated as he held up scraps of cloth for sale in front of a young man cornered in the alley.

Yet under his tattered clothes, Matthias held enough denarii to keep a family housed and fed for years. Over time, working to be unnoticed, Matthias had become an expert in disguise in the streets of Jerusalem.

"Matthias, next time give me a warning. I was going to push you aside as another beggar!" Mark looked up, straining to make out Matthias's face in the dimming light. "And as for the deal, have you lost your senses? That's a lot of wood for what you offer."

Dressed in a clean white-and-blue tunic, Mark was a stark contrast to Matthias. He held out his hands and inspected the cloth that Matthias presented, facilitating Matthias's disguise.

Mark thought it odd for Matthias to bargain with such intensity. His casual style was his trademark in Jerusalem, but today he was determined and direct. Mark's partners knew this request for building wood was special. They also understood not to ask too many questions.

In the end, they accommodated his passionate bargaining out of respect for Matthias, a man whom so many times in that past had ensured there were profits to share for seller and buyer.

"We are going to lose money on this deal!"

"Mark, how many times have I guaranteed you a fat and quick profit? Today I am asking you to give a little; you know that I am making no profit on this deal."

"All right, just this once. Promise me on Abraham's tomb you will not tell anyone the price we negotiated. Three hundred drachma it is."

"Thank you, Mark. You have my trust and, when necessary, my sword."

"Let's pray it never comes to that. It's hard enough to make a living with Herod's and Roman taxes."

"Someday Yahweh will deliver us the Messiah and we'll rule over the Romans for a change." Matthias laughed as he shook hands with Mark.

"Someday, Matthias, someday."

As Matthias walked back to the dilapidated inn that he had made his home, he sensed something odd was happening in the streets of Jerusalem. He recognized familiar faces looking at him with open recognition and a slight nod.

'There are too many in the streets who know who I am. It is no longer safe to be in Jerusalem. But Susanna will not want to move again.'

Matthias continued to walk past the inn, arriving in an alley several blocks away. Here was a young man clothed very similarly to Matthias, with a hood covering his face.

Matthias looked sternly at Jonathan. "The price of lumber is set, Jonathan. It's three hundred drachmas for all the cedar you should need."

"My thanks, Matthias. You know the price would have been double if I had asked for the lumber. Rebuilding the old inn is getting to be known. It makes for a poor negotiating position."

Matthias hesitated but finally admitted he was right. "I'm proud of you, Jonathan. You've come far. Susanna talks about you and wonders how Sara and Mara are doing."

"Thanks to you, they are secure and at peace. I had doubts that my mother could bear to see the inn resurrected after my father's death. My mother and I had a long talk about how my father would want us to be safe. I think she's looking forward to having a real home in the future. Mara is excited about the new people she'll meet."

Suddenly, Matthias turned his head toward the alley entrance. Dim shadows appeared at the head of the alley and then he ducked as a bronze knife flashed past him and stuck in a corner post, vibrating harmlessly.

Five young men approached. Matthias recognized the gang of thugs who had chased Jonathan into a similar alley many years before, the day he took him under his protection. But it was different now. The boys were now men and much more dangerous. And he and Jonathan were alone.

"Barabbas, you fool, you never learn, do you?" demanded Matthias as he pulled his short sword from underneath his cloak. From the corner of his eye, Matthias watched as Jonathan reached for his dagger.

"Don't do anything, Jonathan," Matthias ordered. "These thugs have been pursuing us for months. They seem to believe you owe them a debt."

"I paid my debt to them years ago. They keep demanding more." Jonathan was furious about being extorted.

With a smirk on his face, Barabbas announced, "We just want to relieve you of your burdens, Matthias. We'll take that pouch and Jonathan's as well." Barabbas nodded, and his four companions unveiled their weapons, three short swords. All had knives.

Matthias clenched his sword and balanced his legs. Raising his voice, he demanded, "Leave now and no one will be hurt. Stay and someone will likely die today."

There was a rush as the thieves charged forward. For a moment time slowed. Matthias watched the men step toward Jonathan. Jonathan was no threat to the thieves, but he couldn't leave the boy alone. He did the only thing he could—he screamed.

"Damn your souls!" Raising his sword, Matthias shrieked like a madman. When he reached the first of the five, he suddenly lunged forward, struck the outstretched weapon, and spun around to strike the back of the thug's shoulders.

Startled, Jonathan looked at Matthias and took up the war cry as he ran at the four thugs. "God's wrath!" screamed Jonathan.

Barabbas motioned the others towards Matthias as he approached Jonathan. Raising his knife, Jonathan hesitated, swallowed, and then rushed toward Barabbas. Turning to avoid the knife, Barabbas twirled the sword in his right hand and struck Jonathan with the broadside of his sword, directly across the back of his head. Dazed, Jonathan moaned and collapsed.

Matthias ducked low and avoided the second thief's wild swing over his head. Reacting instinctively, Matthias thrust his sword upward to catch the thief in the hip. As the thief fell over, he dropped his sword and grabbed his hip in agony. Jumping up, Matthias turned and faced the two remaining thieves.

"Which one of you wants to die first?!?" Matthias screamed.

The two remaining thugs split and circled Matthias. The first lunged at Matthias with his knife, thrusting it toward his midsection. Matthias turned and struck his assailant in the shoulder. Gestas, the second man, maneuvered behind him and in a desperate move threw his knife at Matthias's back. The knife struck hard into his lower backside, just to the right of his spine and liver as Matthias struck at the torso of the first assailant.

Screaming in pain, Matthias turned and dropped to his knees. Matthias was kneeling when he blindly thrust his sword outward, striking the second approaching thief in the stomach just as he raised his sword to finish Matthias.

"I got him!" Shouted Getas, standing behind Mathias.

A groggy Jonathan cried out. "Matthias!"

"I have you now, you little bastard!" Barabbas raised his sword to strike Jonathan.

Without warning, a tall Roman officer sitting atop a huge black horse shouted, "Stop this now! We will cut you down where you stand. And any that may survive will be jailed until you rot." He turned and shouted orders to his soldiers. "Move into the alley!"

In a moment of brief and deafening silence, Barabbas looked behind him, and Jonathan saw genuine fear on his face.

"Stop where you stand!" the Roman officer ordered. Twenty Roman soldiers, guards just relieved from watch duty in King Herod's palace, poured into the alley.

Bleeding from the head and dazed, Jonathan blinked to clear his eyes enough to look around. He couldn't find

Matthias or Barabbas. But he cleared his eyes enough to see the Roman officer and recognized the fortress quartermaster officer. And then Jonathan passed out.

The three wounded thugs lay on the ground, surrounded by the Roman guards. Three soldiers forced Gestas to the ground, taking his sword and knife. "Bind their wounds and take them to the stockade," ordered Cassius. "We've been looking for these bastards for months."

Pointing to Jonathan, Cassius ordered his soldiers to take the young beggar to the temple for his wounds. "The Jewish rabbis will know how to deal with him."

A soldier approached Cassius, "Standard, two escaped. We think one was the leader. He was carrying a sword. The other looked like another beggar. I think he was wounded."

Looking up at his squad, Cassius was angry. "You need to move faster when the order is given! Someday your lives will depend upon speed." Cassius knew his men were tired at the end of their day, but he also knew he couldn't afford hesitation from his soldiers. "Move out, now!"

PHYSICIAN

Matthias limped into the inn, blood dripping on the floor through his dirty tunic. Susanna looked up and screamed. "What have you done now, brother?" Matthias dropped to the floor.

Susanna yelled for help. She lifted his tunic and saw the blood-soaked undershirt. Susanna did the only thing she could think of . . . she dragged Matthias into his bed. He was just conscious enough to lean on his sister for help until he collapsed on his stomach and passed out. Wrapping his wound the best she could, Susanna immediately ran out of the inn to muster Matthias's underground friends. She needed help to find Jonathan and a doctor for Matthias.

After running through the streets of Jerusalem for a half-hour, Susanna finally found Levi, an old friend of Matthias from his early days of fighting Romans as a Zealot. Levi was able to quickly locate another friend and former Zealot, Shulman, and his son Kantor, to help search for Jonathan and find a physician. An hour later, the men had located Jonathan in the temple. With an offering of a few denarii, the rabbis were more than willing to be rid of the unconscious beggar. Levi and Shulman carried Jonathan and loaded him onto the back of a donkey, while Kantor went in search of a visiting physician from Assyria, a young man named Luke, who was no friend of the Romans or King Herod.

Returning to the inn, Levi and Shulman found Susanna sobbing and holding Matthias. Levi was able to lift Jonathan and carry him into another room and lay him on a cot next to a burnt doorway. As Jonathan and Matthias lay unconscious in adjacent rooms, Susanna stood between the two, terrified of losing both that night. Levi nodded to her and hurried off to locate Kantor and the physician.

Susanna hovered over both Jonathan and Matthias throughout the night. Simultaneously praying and crying, Susanna knew they needed more help than she could give them. Matthias awoke near dawn, wondering where he was. Susanna rushed to the door, dropped to her knees, held him in her arms, and cried with relief.

"Let go before you strangle me," groaned Matthias. Susanna smiled as Matthias drifted back into unconsciousness.

An hour later, the young Greek doctor knocked on the door of the inn. He looked down at Matthias and saw the blood soaking through the bandages. Luke grimaced as he unwrapped the bandages from Matthias' wound.

"Rumors of the fight have already spread through the city. Roman soldiers are searching for anyone involved," Luke explained.

"Please help my brother! I've done my best, but I fear he's near death. There's a young man, Jonathan, in the other room. He's unconscious, too. I think he's been hit in the head."

Luke looked up at Susanna and saw that her tears obscured her brown eyes. "I'm told you are Susanna."

"Yes, and you're the Syrian?" said Susanna as she gripped her prayer shawl.

"My name is Luke, I live and study in Antioch, but I'm Greek. I'm here in Jerusalem to study under the physician Rabbi Ishmael. Do not worry, I have no loyalty to either the Romans or King Herod. Whatever I do here tonight is done in secret."

"Please help him," Susanna pleaded. Matthias was shaking, sweating profusely.

"I will do the best I can, Susanna. I've been told he is a good man, though a bit mysterious. Now please get me wine and oil. I need to clean and seal his wound."

Luke worked for two hours mending Matthias's wound, and then went to Jonathan's room and wrapped his head. By the time he returned to Matthias, it was well past midday. Luke had been able to stop the bleeding and close the knife wound. After cleaning and sewing the incision, the sun's light was dimming, announcing the end of another day.

"Keep him warm and I'll come by later tonight to see how they are both doing. If he wakes, try to make him drink as much as he can. Soup would be best. Jonathan is another story. I did the best I could, but he has a serious head injury. And Susanna, whatever you do, keep them both quiet for a least two weeks."

Susanna hesitated, her eyes still wet from tears and then asked, "Are they going to die?"

"I hope not . . . they are both strong. The knife missed Matthias's liver and kidney, and his bleeding stopped. But if he starts moving it may reopen the wound. Next time I may not be able to stop it. You must make him rest. Understand?"

Susanna murmured, "My brother is a good man with a kind heart. It's up to God to save him now."

"Shalom, Susanna, sleep while you can. They'll need your help when they wake."

JONATHAN

During the previous night, Levi had stopped at Sara's apartment to tell her about the fight and Jonathan's condition. Fighting off her worst fears, Sara left with Levi to find her son. She knew that Susanna needed her support, just as much as Jonathan and Matthias.

The sun finally appeared through the window, announcing the end of the long night that threatened to be the last for

Jonathan and Matthias. Beams of new daylight caught Sara as she held Jonathan's hand.

When the sun's light hit Jonathan's face, he stirred, then jolted upward. He grimaced as though a sharp knife was splitting his brain. The intense pain from his migraine was excruciating, causing him to vomit into a nearby bowl. Carefully lowering himself onto the bed, he squinted at Sara but said nothing for what seemed an eternity. Pain reflected on both of their faces.

"Stay quiet, Jonathan. Matthias is alive but is in bad shape, but God has given him another day."

Jonathan sighed and said nothing. He finally closed his eyes, blocking out the light which was causing his throbbing headache to get worse. Tears began to flow from his shut eyes, releasing the fear and heartache that had overwhelmed him upon waking. Sara struggled to maintain her composure, realizing that a dark fear ran deep within Jonathan. She sat there quietly holding his hand, sitting across from Matthias's room, praying that God could save these two men from their wounds.

"I love you, my son," Sara whispered as Jonathan faded back to sleep.

AWAKE

When Jonathan awoke again, the room was dark. Another day had passed. The blackness overwhelmed him, pushing his consciousness back into the obscure corners of his mind.

Where was he? Where were his father and mother? Why did his head feel like it would explode at any moment?

Slowly, he remembered the events of the night which brought him back to the present. He and Matthias had been attacked. He knew that he was still in his room at the inn and Matthias was sleeping in the room across from him. But Susanna and Sara were gone. Instinctively, Jonathan reached out from his cot, wanting to touch Matthias as he slept, needing confirmation his mentor and friend was still alive. But the distance between rooms was too far, and every time Jonathan tried to sit up, the room spun in circles and he felt sick to his stomach.

Lying back, he tried to make sense of events. Memories of his dying father brought additional fears. He began to wonder what sins he had committed to make God so angry with him. Shuddering uncontrollably, he reached outward to hold his father. His father's image hovered in his consciousness.

Trembling, he put his hands over his face and felt sweat pouring down his forehead and cheeks. A fever? He fought to maintain his grip on his senses but again lost control. Alone, he began to cry in anger and frustration.

"Not again. God, why have you allowed this cruelty? What have I done to you? Why?"

Jonathan was near the end of his hope. Pain had led him to dark alleys in his mind where hope was not welcome. He could not bear to lose someone he loved again, and the stench of fear and death filled the air. In the darkness, despair and anger were all that remained.

"Damn you all. Why? This is not what I wanted!"

Jonathan struggled to compose himself and his thoughts. Sobbing, he cried out again, "Lord, I am not a strong man. I need help. I am alone, tired. You've won. I'm broken. I am begging for Your help. Lord, I ask that You give me the breath of Your courage. Help me, Lord."

Jonathan battled his fears throughout the night, his body thrashing as the fears inside of him tormented his soul. He reached the point of exhaustion just before daybreak. At last, he lay quietly and yielded to his exhaustion.

"*Your Father loves you; His love brings strength,*" whispered the night wind.

"What? Who is there?" whispered Jonathan.

The wind whistled through the window.

"*You are stronger than you know. Your Father loves you. Honor Him,*" repeated the voice.

Too exhausted to continue the strange dialogue, Jonathan reached again for Matthias, then overextended and fell out of his cot. Laying on the ground he crawled to Matthias's bed until he lost consciousness on the cold floor, holding tightly onto Matthias's blanket.

The night passed in an instant and Jonathan woke to the echoes of the voice in his head. He staggered upward, attempting to find his balance, but fell backward landing hard on his knees. His head nearly exploded. Rising slowly as the shooting pain subsided, he saw the first glimpse of light through the broken window, and soon the dawn began to dominate over the darkness. A beam of morning light shot past the outline of city buildings to illuminate his room.

Bewildered, he thought what he had heard the previous night was only a dream. Perhaps he had fallen asleep for an instant and was immediately caught in a dream.

"His love brings strength?" repeated Jonathan. He had no idea what that meant, or how it would help him. He was still alone, but somehow less afraid.

In that moment, Jonathan understood something was different. The sun cascaded onto his face and instantly gave him a glimpse of hope. Perhaps the darkness would eventually fade. He peered into the adjoining room and saw Matthias sleeping, his chest rising and falling heavily as he labored for air.

Jonathan returned to his cot and collapsed again into a deep slumber.

CASSIUS

Night brought little respite from the day. Arising from his bed slowly, Cassius contorted his movements to minimize muscle pain, his disorientation increased by weariness. Cassius knew he needed more sleep. For the past three months, he could only find it in short segments, often broken by muscle cramps and images of the black-haired servant girl. His body craved the surrender of sleep, but his mind buffered his tranquility, demanding that he bring life to the faint picture of Mary.

The door creaked open, and his steward broke the silence. "Standard, we have bread and dates for breakfast."

Cassius looked up and moaned. "What bloody time is it?"

"It's an hour before sunrise, sir. You gave the order to wake you so you could observe the morning guard shift."

"I'm up," Cassius lied as he lay in his rack for a few more minutes. Slowly flexing his calf and thigh muscles, he started working the pains from his legs and shoulders. Five minutes later, he was up and dressed, walking into the guards' dining area to pick up his breakfast.

Without fail, Mary was on his mind each night. But she was also with him during the day. For the past several months, images of her working in the palace broke his concentration, and he found himself shaking his head to clear the thoughts of her. Because she worked in the palace, Cassius was also concerned that her beauty would cause her to be abused by palace royalty or his fellow guards.

Cassius was also keenly aware that Mary was troubled. Rumors in the palace said she was possessed by demons. He clearly understood that a Roman officer having a relationship with a palace slave of Herod's, and one who was possessed by demons, was grounds for a demotion to a common foot soldier. His own impulsiveness might destroy the very dreams he and Bracus had of joining the Roman Legions. So, though he knew he should keep his distance, he had a hard time staying away from the palace and Mary.

But something was driving him he could not explain, something deeper in Mary. He couldn't explain why he continued to pursue this dangerous relationship with her, but he could not stop. Though she seemed disinterested in his small talk and nods, she did not dismiss his attention. Twice she smiled as she nodded and walked away. Cassius was perplexed yet intrigued.

Finally, Cassius made up his mind. He knew he had to master the realm of sleep and clear his head. His plan was simple. He physically drove himself to exhaustion. Surely, as soon as he collapsed into his bed, he would find sweet relief.

The morning started with riding Venti and training other horses for four hours. At midday, he challenged his men to sword and spear exercises for two hours. By late afternoon he started running and finally stopped at the point of near collapse. His goal was just one night of uninterrupted, blissful sleep.

Falling into an exhausted slumber that night, he finally achieved peace. He awoke the next morning with a clear mind, refreshed, and with new courage to confront the conflict between his head and heart.

After washing, he dressed and headed to check on his guards. Thirty minutes later he walked through the halls of Herod's palace.

"Wake up, Cephas. You look drowsy this morning," Cassius called out.

The startled guard stood up straight and saluted Cassius. "Yes, Standard. You're up early this morning."

"Just making my rounds. What hour do they serve breakfast to King Herod?"

"I can smell the bread in the kitchens, sir. Usually, they start serving within the next hour."

"Make sure you are diligent, Cephas. Your watch is almost over."

The guard stood taller as Cassius walked past him into the palace, heading in the direction of the kitchens.

It was apprehension that upset Cassius's stomach, despite his hunger. Despite his nervousness, he walked straight to the kitchens and toward the smell of fresh bread. Turning the last corner, Cassius spotted two women preparing trays for Herod's table. At that point, his last remnant of courage left him.

Joanna looked up from her tray of wine, olive oil, figs, melons, and fresh bread to see him standing in the hallway.

"Isn't that your Roman officer, Mary?" asked Joanna.

Mary looked up to see Cassius, standing outside the kitchen. Looking down at the tray, she smiled, then snapped back at Joanna, "He's *not* my Roman soldier. Please, you'll get us all in trouble."

Mary looked up at Cassius again and waved him into the kitchen. "I assume you are dying of starvation again, Standard?" quipped Mary. "Don't just stand there. We have extra this morning. Joanna will make a tray for you. I'm leaving before someone crashes into my food tray and I get into trouble again." Mary brushed past Cassius, catching her side against his arm. Cassius could smell the fragrance of her hair as she passed. "Go on, she won't bite you. But I may, I have demons." Mary smiled as she exited the room.

Mary dropped her head for a moment, pleased that Cassius had returned, even if it was only for a few moments.

Cassius walked into the kitchen and started to thank Joanna, but without any thought of self-control, he turned to look at Mary walking away.

"Thank you. You both are kind," Cassius finally managed to say to Joanna.

Joanna set a plate for Cassius of bread, figs, olive oil, and melons. "There's fresh milk in the pitcher if you'd like."

As Joanna picked up her food tray and started to head to Herod's table, she stopped briefly to look at Cassius. His curly black hair, olive complexion, handsome face, and chiseled features made him look more like a statue than a soldier. Joanna saw in his hazel eyes an uncommon softness and intelligence. She realized Cassius wasn't just another heartless Roman soldier. She could see there was something different, something that she couldn't pinpoint.

Momentarily breathless, Joanna hesitated and then walked across the kitchen and gave Cassius a smile. When she was around the corner, Joanna stopped for air. She shook her head as she realized that something was happening, something that she could not articulate or control. She felt a connection between Mary, Cassius, and herself that was important, and she couldn't explain why.

THE NEXT SUNRISE

Mary cleaned pots in Herod's kitchen for an hour as dawn rose over Jerusalem's houses and shops, delivering another new day to the holy city. She raised her hand and opened the curtains of the lone stone window in the kitchen. Gazing out, she held up her hand to block the brilliant sun from blinding her view of Jerusalem. She continued to look through her fingers at the crimson lights spiking across the rooftops of the city. Light came like a tidal wave, flooding away the darkness of night and announcing a new day. For a moment, the beauty of the scene encouraged her heart to hope for a better day. Mary rarely dared to believe in a happy future. Hope was too transient, too effervescent to believe that it was real.

Joanna, her companion since being sold into Herold's servitude, was sitting beside her, drying the breakfast pots. She also noticed the brilliant morning sun, sighed, and continued working.

"I've seen him looking at you with those cow eyes again, Mary. By Moses's beard, that man is smitten. He sees through the smudges on your face and looks for your eyes every time he walks by. Besides . . ." Joanna poked Mary who almost dropped the clay pot, "he has kind eyes."

"Stop it, Joanna. You are one to talk. I've seen the same cow eyes you've given to Chuza. You know both relationships are forbidden, especially with Herod's house manager. We'll be beaten," sighed Mary. "And you know that being seen with a Roman soldier, much less a Roman officer, could get me much worse . . ." Mary sighed softly again. "No matter how handsome and clumsy he is. And, yes, he does have kind eyes."

Joanna smiled. "Someday life will be different." In her heart, she somehow knew this was true. Something important was coming.

Chapter 8

TIME TO HEAL

27 AD

JERUSALEM

"I'm going to work tomorrow. It's time," Matthias declared, sitting in the half-finished tavern dining hall. New lumber had been delivered and stacked in the corner and Matthias found that the stacks made convenient benches.

"Matthias, it's only been three months," Jonathan protested. "You can barely move, much less avoid the Romans or Barabbas and his thieves."

"I'll start slowly, cautiously. I appreciate your concern but the opportunities on the streets won't wait for us," Matthias quietly replied.

"Can you wait at least another two weeks?"

"No, there's something brewing, Jonathan. I can feel it. We need to get started with the construction now."

Jonathan understood what Matthias was telling him. Something was changing, although he couldn't put a finger on it. Maybe the attack by Barabbas was a warning that Jerusalem was destined to become even more volatile.

"Matthias, I'll support your decisions. I know about the time my father saved you in Magdalena when the Romans attacked. And you've saved me twice from Barabbas. I am here. I will always stand with you."

Matthias stood up, stunned by Jonathan's admission of trust. Since the attack, something had changed in Jonathan. Matthias thought he sensed a softening in his partner. "All right. But that was a long time ago. What happened is long past. Let's leave it behind us. We have work to do, and you have an inn to rebuild."

Matthias walked across the room and sat down on the table, holding a steaming cup of broth. "You'll need to design the inn to look different than it was. It can't look or feel the same. If it reminds customers of the old inn, you'll never escape the past. And you've got to be prepared—someone will always bring up the past. Create an inn where people will talk about the future."

"I understand, Matthias. Now we have a new job. Construction. You're a part of this, too. For me and Father."

Jonathan clearly understood the irony. From the ashes of the inn where his father died, he was attempting to rebuild a profitable life for himself, his mother, and his sister. Yet he also knew that ghosts from his past would challenge him. The fear of failure still terrified him.

MARY

It was late afternoon when Cassius entered Herod's palace, turning right into the massive courtyard filled with palm trees and desert plants. The afternoon sun had set behind the 20-foot walls of the palace, cooling the courtyard from the heat of the day. As he walked across the open space and into the hallways to check on his guards, per his usual routine, Cassius heard the muffled sound of a woman screaming.

Initially, Cassius thought it was one of the maids being punished for some minor infraction of house rules. He decided to avoid the situation; there was nothing he could do to help Herod's servants. But when the screaming intensified, he could no longer ignore the distress of the woman. He ran toward the desperate sounds, turning the corner of the hallway and suddenly stopped and grabbed the hilt of his sword. Tavian, one of his guards who had just been relieved of his night-guard duty, was trying to drag a palace servant into a storeroom. In her fight, she sank to the floor, kicking Tavian's shins in self-defense.

Cassius shouted, "Tavian, stop, now!"

Tavian turned to face Cassius and smiled. "Spoils of the conquerors, Standard!"

Cassius drew his sword, strode up to Tavian, and grabbed the neck of his cloak. With one quick thrust, Cassius pulled Tavian away from the woman, throwing him against the opposite wall. Tavian hit with a thud. His head bounced off the stone and he collapsed.

Cassius bellowed, "Guards! To me now!"

Turning, he looked down and saw the servant crying, curled into a ball as though she expected to be beaten again. For the first time, Cassius saw that the small servant was Mary. He had not recognized her screams. The sight horrified Cassius. He had seen so much violence and death serving in the Roman Legions. Like many Roman soldiers, Cassius had almost become numb to the violence. He accepted it as part of his life.

But now as he looked down on Mary, crying and shaking, the face of brutality became real. This was personal. Kneeling next to Mary, he took off his crimson cape and placed it around her shoulders.

"I'm sorry, I'm so sorry," he said. "This will never happen again; you have my word. No one in this palace will ever hurt you again."

It took a few minutes for Mary to calm down. Taking the cape, she wrapped it around her body. Through her jet-black hair, she spoke, "Th-th-thank you."

Cassius stood straight as his soldiers arrived. "Sergeant, take Tavian back to the fortress. He attacked one of Herod's servants. I'll see to his punishment myself. Then come back here immediately. I'll stay until you return."

After the guards dragged Tavian away, Cassius turned and knelt next to Mary, "Excuse my clumsiness, I'm a simple soldier. Are you hurt?"

"No. I'm . . . I'm . . . I'm OK. I'm not hurt. Thank you . . . for saving me. Please don't apologize or feel clumsy around me, Standard." Behind Mary's tears, her stare was intense.

Cassius took a deep breath and looked her in the eyes. Her unusual hazel green eyes, offset by her jet-black hair and flawless complexion, once again stunned him stupid. She offered a small smile and Cassius couldn't speak. He had never seen a woman as beautiful and graceful as Mary. He knelt there, with nothing to say.

It was Mary who offered him a way back to sanity. "I've been rude to you. Perhaps we can call a truce."

Cassius tried to muster a causal smile, but it came out more of a grimace. "We have an agreement then. I will look in on you from time to time when I'm in the palace. That is, if you will permit."

"As long as we are discreet, Standard." Mary stood and looked directly at Cassius. "Thank you again." Mary handed Cassius his cape back, straightened her tunic, and smiled at him as she walked away, looking braver than she felt.

Cassius tried hard not to stare as she left, but his notorious iron will and self-control failed him . . . again.

It was a week before Cassius ran across Mary again, this time in the kitchen helping with the evening meal. Mary looked up and Cassius froze. Only her quick smile freed him.

Cassius nodded and decided to try again after the king's evening meal when she might be less busy. Stepping into the kitchen, Cassius looked at Mary, watching her pick up an overflowing plate of fruit and say something to Joanna. Joanna, glancing at Cassius, gave a quick wink, grabbed Mary's plate and walked away, leaving Cassius and Mary alone.

"It is good to see you again, Mary. Are you well?" blurted out Cassius. Mary smiled at his awkwardness. She replied that she was and asked him a simple question about his morning which led to them talking about life in Jerusalem. Before Cassius realized it, he and Mary were laughing, enjoying each other's company.

"I must go before anyone sees us. Thank you for coming by," she said.

Cassius nodded his understanding. "Until next time."

The next encounter came with Joanna, just outside the kitchen. Dropping a metal plate of leftover fruit in front of Cassius, Joanna created an opportunity to talk to him. When Cassius stopped to help recover the scattered fruit, she spoke quietly, "Standard, you are becoming well-known in the palace. I believe you have a good heart, but your eyes betray you, even when you try to hide your feelings."

Taken aback, Cassius looked at her, "Thank you. It seems that you are a good friend to Mary."

"Yes, we've been roommates since she came to the palace as a servant ten years ago.

"Mary speaks highly of you. She is also special to me. Her wounds are deep, but I see a spark of light in her eyes when she talks about you."

"She talks about me?" Cassius hid a smile.

"Yes, but I must warn you. On occasions, Mary has fits where she faints and sometimes shivers. Some think she is possessed by demons. I just need to let you know, so you'll be prepared."

Cassius looked at Joanna intently as he helped her finish piling the fruit on the tray. "Thank you for telling me, Joanna. I've heard the rumors. I assure you, I'm not frightened by what you say, though I am thankful I can bring some brightness to her eyes."

"I see the same in you, Standard. You both have some special purpose. I pray you can protect it."

"Yes, it can be a cruel world. We need to hold onto the things that are precious, Joanna. Thank you for trusting me."

Each new encounter with Mary caused a chain reaction that seemed to alter his soul. Cassius found himself falling deeper into a strange new world. The constant guilt of Bracus's death was slowly melting away. Mary's effect on Cassius was transforming him. His pain was slowly being replaced by another emotion—one that, at first, was just a fleeting thought—but then it grew to a frightening and seductive emotion: hope. For the first time in a long time, he believed there could be a future without pain, either his own or that which he saw in others.

Cassius imagined himself spending a whole day with Mary in Gethsemane, a thought that frequently captivated his mind. He also visualized a life with someone like her, a woman he could love beyond question, free from obligatory duties and critical eyes.

Cassius was also gaining confidence with each new encounter. He could sense that Mary was starting to see him as a friend rather than just a Roman soldier, an enemy. Despite her reluctance and initial aloofness, Cassius believed she was beginning to trust him and enjoy his companionship. At each new meeting, Mary's smile seemed more genuine, her laughter more frequent.

But as his relationship with Mary grew, in the back of Cassius's mind grew another haunting thought. *'What if I lose her? I can't. I just can't.'* For the first time in his life, Cassius was terrified.

JONATHAN

"Blast my clumsiness!" yelled Jonathan as he dropped the nails for a second time. Tired and sweating, he bent to recover the scattered nails he needed to finish the partition wall inside the inn.

Just then, Jonathan saw the shadow of a man approaching him through the rubble of the old inn. He stood up, holding his hammer tightly, ready for any surprise.

"You dropped the nails because you're tired. The word on the street is that this inn will never be rebuilt. You definitely can't do this alone.

"For a fair wage, I believe I can help you. I'm a carpenter by trade. My name is Jason."

Despite his youth, Jason had hollowed cheeks and dark circles under his eyes. His matted hair and unkept clothes told of nights sleeping in alleys, most likely avoiding Romans and thieves. But most of all, Jason needed a bath and clean clothes.

'*Without the grace of God, I was that man.*' Without the help of Matthias, Jonathan saw himself in that young man's place.

Memories flooded Jonathan's mind. He thought back to a time after his father died, when he was living off the streets, trading what little he could scrounge or steal, doing anything to make enough money to buy food for his mother, sister, and himself.

Looking back to the man standing before him, Jonathan asked, "What experience do you have?"

"I've been working construction since I was a small boy. I was apprenticed to John the master builder who was killed when scaffolding fell two years ago in the temple."

Jonathan nodded, remembering that day. He had heard about the accident. But he hesitated as he thought about his father working in the temple. '*That could have been Father.*'

Jason continued, "I've been doing odd jobs since then. And besides, you need someone strong. That old man you have helping you isn't enough."

Angered at Jason's casual insult, Jonathan shot back, "That old man can sustain a day's labor in the quarries and not complain. He's stronger than he looks, and he's none of your concern." Calming himself, Jonathan paused. "We can pay a denarius per day. It's a temporary job. Clean yourself and be here after dawn. We'll provide a lunch meal, and you can stay here in the unfinished area of the inn starting tomorrow. It will be safer than out in the streets."

Jason grinned. "In the morning, then."

On his first day, Jason showed himself to be an eager and hardworking carpenter. With regular meals and a bath, Jason no longer looked like a roughneck or vagabond. Jonathan began to feel as though he had been given a chance to repay his debt for surviving.

Matthias approached Jonathan with concern. "Jon, you've been working too hard. I agree that we need help."

Jonathan looked up and nodded to Matthias.

"But hiring this young apprentice? Before he came here, he was living in the alleys. The word on the streets is that he isn't to be trusted."

"Matthias, I gave him my word that he would have an opportunity here. I'm not going to quit on him without even seeing his work. We need help and skilled labor is hard to find because of the temple work. You know that."

Matthias was about to retort when Jonathan interjected, "Matthias, I gave him my word."

Jonathan and Matthias looked at each other with weary eyes; they both knew they needed help.

"All right, Jon, but let's keep a close eye on the boy. I don't trust him."

"Agreed," responded Jonathan.

He'd already suspected he was taking a risk on Jason. There was something not right with him. Even after they worked together for two months, with Jason proving that he was skilled and hardworking, Jonathan was still uncertain. Something about the young man unsettled Jonathan.

As the work progressed with rebuilding the inn, his fears grew. Jonathan's temper flared. He often snapped at Sara or Mara. Realizing he was falling back into who he had been before his head injury, harder and more bitter, Jonathan tried to keep away from his family, sleeping in the extra room in the back of the unfinished inn. His fears chased him as the demons of the past haunted him. Failure was a constant threat he could not ignore.

THREE MONTHS LATER

"Jason, you cut these boards too short again!" Jonathan was seeing more and more discrepancies in Jason's work. The tongue-and-groove fittings needed for square edges were not fitting correctly. Besides that, the expensive lumber was starting to disappear faster than it was being used. And on top of all that, there were times when Jason left early, usually without notice.

He finally reached out to Matthias for advice, even though he had been tightlipped about Jason. "Keep an eye on him, Jonathan. He has a drinking problem."

By the end of the next month, Jonathan suspected Jason was drinking heavily, too often to be trusted. Another week passed and Jason's behavior continued to degrade. Finally, Jason missed a workday and slinked back to the inn after dark looking sullen and dehydrated.

"I don't want to hear your excuses, Jason. Get cleaned up, have a good's night rest, and be ready for work tomorrow at sunrise!"

The next day Jonathan ventured into the market to obtain Passover supplies, wondering what to do about Jason. He looked for Mark the merchant in the crowded market and eventually found him.

"My friend Jon, it's good to see you. Good Sabbath."

"Good Sabbath, Mark, how is your family?"

"Getting fat and sassy. Bertha is with another child, and the kids are growing like weeds. Jonathan, you need a family, can I loan you two of my kids?"

Jonathan smiled at Mark. "I can't afford your family, you keep multiplying!"

"I was searching for you today. A young man came to me to buy wine, and not my best wine either. It was strange because he wished to trade cedar lumber for the wine."

Jonathan hesitated, anticipating the worst. "Yes?"

"When I sold the cedar to Matthias last fall, I thought it would be used to rebuild the inn," Mark continued. "But when I found your young apprentice negotiating to sell some of this lumber for himself, I was concerned and thought I'd talk to you."

Jonathan looked down to hide his anger, frustration in his eyes and clenched fists. "Thank you so much for letting me know. You are a good friend, Mark. I'll deal with it and let Matthias know what is happening. Can you tell me how much of the lumber you bought back? I'd like the chance to rebuy the lumber."

Seeing Jonathan's uncharacteristic anger, Mark surmised he may have started a series of unfortunate outcomes for the young man. Mark chuckled to relieve the tension. "For the price of the wine I sold to him I'd be glad to give it back to you. Come over tomorrow and you can pick up the lumber."

"Thank you, Mark. As I said, you're a good friend and I won't forget how you've helped us." Jonathan nodded to Mark, then turned back toward the inn.

Twenty minutes later, Jonathan slammed the inn's door and yelled, "Damnation, Jason! You stole from me."

Jason started to protest until Matthias entered the room. "What's going on, Jon?"

"I just talked to Mark in the market. It seems we are short of lumber, Matthias, as you suspected. Only now do I understand why. Jason sold part of the wood to buy wine. To drown his troubles despite how it hurt us and the opportunities we've given him!"

Jason looked up at Jonathan as though he were a trapped man. "I'm sorry, sir. I'm sorry that I—"

"Get out, Jason. Now! Never set foot on this property again," shouted Jonathan.

As Jason ran out the door, Matthias walked up to Jonathan. "We suspected he had problems, Jon. What are you going to do?"

"Mark has agreed to give us the wood for the price of the cheap wine Jason stole. We'll recover. Then I'll charge Jason's wages for the price we had to rebuy the wine!"

"You know he doesn't have the money, even with the wages you owe him," answered Matthias.

"That's his problem now, he can rot in debtor's prison for all I care. Matthias, we took him in, and he stole from us!"

Running from the inn, Jason stumbled across the street and continued to run through the streets of Jerusalem, still half-drunk. Swearing to himself, Jason fought his rising guilt and shame. His demons—temptation, drinking, jealousy— had ruined another opportunity.

He screamed at himself, "You idiot! You drunkard! You did it again. You want me to suffer!"

Arriving at sunset in a back alley, Jason stumbled across his own feet and fell, his body answering his self-loathing accusations. He curled himself up into a ball and sobbed, homeless again.

'You'll go to prison this time. You idiot. You'll likely die there.' He shuddered at the thought of his inevitable future.

MATTHIAS

"It's done, Matthias. I have signed the debt petition against Jason. The Romans are looking for him now."

A week had passed since they discovered Jason's treachery. Matthias looked down and frowned. "Prison is a hard thing, Jonathan. Most don't survive."

"We didn't ask him to steal. We gave him a chance. He only hurt himself."

Matthias only shook his head.

"Anyway, Matthias, you were right, we need help finishing the inn."

Matthias didn't respond to Jonathan immediately, but paused and then spoke, "I might have an answer."

Two days later, Matthias walked the streets early in the morning, dressed as a beggar, hiding from Roman soldiers and inquiring eyes. As he turned a corner, he stopped and watched a rabbi for several minutes. The rabbi had been pretending to shop for fresh fruit and bread, typically a task of the Temple servants. Satisfied that the rabbi was waiting for someone, Matthias slowly walked up behind the man.

"Can you spare a coin for this poor beggar?" Matthias murmured.

The rabbi turned, frowned at Matthias, and asked. "Are you a friend of the Temple?"

"I am your servant," Matthias responded. The rabbi walked away from the crowd and Matthias followed.

"I am Matthias, the man you seek, the one who can solve many problems," Matthias affirmed once outside of hearing from strangers in the market.

After carefully looking over Matthias, the rabbi reached inside his cloak and pulled out a crumpled scroll. "This letter is for you. It's from Nicodemus the Pharisee. He asks that you read it and give it back to me. Afterward, if you agree, I'll give you a denarius. It will look like I'm helping a poor beggar."

Matthias opened the letter and read the contract, which requested a hundred unblemished sheep, two hundred doves, and thirty young oxen for the altar sacrifices. Matthias looked up at the rabbi and nodded in agreement.

"I can arrange these items, but it will take six weeks. It will also cost an extra three hundred denarii for travel expenses and security. These items cannot be found in Jerusalem this late in the spring, in surrounding towns, or within 50 leagues. Especially of the quality the temple priests would accept. I will have to travel far and there are risks on the road. And I'll need one-half the funds up front to pay for travel and merchandise," Matthias finished.

"Agreed," whispered the young rabbi and handed Matthias a denarius. "Come by the outer temple wall tomorrow at noon and we'll fund the trip."

As the rabbi departed, he called back to Matthias, "May God bless you on the Sabbath."

Matthias's walk back to the inn was slow. He noticed an increase in Roman patrols searching merchants and customers. They were obviously looking for someone. More than once, Matthias ducked behind a merchant's stall or into an alley to avoid questioning.

When he returned to the inn, Matthias asked Jonathan to take a break and sit down with him.

"Jon, I've just met with a rabbi from the Temple, and we have a new business deal. But I will need to travel north, perhaps as far as Galilee. This deal promises to more than make up for our losses from Jason and pay for new help. This trip will also allow us to expand our search for good help. But I'll be gone, perhaps up to two months."

Jonathan frowned as he looked down, worry in his eyes. "Two months is a long time, Matthias."

"I understand, but we can make a good profit off this deal with the Temple. I suspected they would need extra sacrificial animals and supplies for the upcoming Passover and the celebrations to honor the completion of the decorations in the Women's Courtyard. They waited until too late to get a reasonable price, so we can make additional profit for the inn."

"I understand, Matthias, but two months is still a long—"

"Yes, but here's my plan. You take over the trading business in Jerusalem while I'm gone. The money you earn will help keep everyone fed and employed. Work on the inn if you can. Start with finding supplies we'll need once we open. Don't fret about getting behind. Take care of Sara, Mara, and Susanna."

"How do we catch up on the building, though?"

"That's the second half of the plan. I'll hire extra workers while I'm in Samaria and Galilee. All the good carpenters in Jerusalem are working in the temple or getting twice the pay on other jobs in the fortress and palaces. We'll pay these new carpenters from the north extra wages to travel to Jerusalem, and they can stay in the inn. It will depend on whom I can find that is trustworthy."

"It's a risk, but it looks like we don't have a choice to turn this down. When do you start your journey?"

"Tomorrow, maybe the next day. I'll need to find a couple of traders to help. The order is large, and we'll need wagons and trained herders. Most I can find along the way, but I'll need guards as well to keep us safe on the way back. I'll find the skilled carpenters and they can help, too."

"Matthias, we've gambled everything on building this inn. I fought so hard to make a life for my mother and Mara. To be honest, I'm worried. We could lose everything; Jason was just one problem. The Romans, the taxes, the thieves who tried to kill us . . . we are taking more and more risks, if we fail, we could lose everything, and it frightens me."

Matthias took him by the shoulders. "Jon, I know you were educated by the rabbis before your father died. Have you gone to the temple to pray, to offer sin offerings, and ask for God's help?"

Jonathan looked up and tears glassed over his eyes. "Not since Father was killed. It seems so fruitless. I miss him so much."

"So does your mother. So do I. We all miss him. But God has a purpose that we don't understand yet. We are all risking so much. Your mother watches you carry your burdens and is afraid someday she'll lose her son, too. Mara is afraid of the future and wonders if her brother can protect her. I walk the streets hiding my identity and praying to God that I can someday repay my debt to your father, a man who was willing to give his life to save mine."

"Jonathan, we are all scared of failure, of the future. The only thing that makes sense is to realize that our God's covenant is real. We need to find Him in moments of peace if we can. Sometimes we find Him in the whispering of the winds. Trust, Jonathan. Believe and trust, and God will answer."

Jonathan looked up at Matthias again, hoping to find certainty in his words, wanting to believe that God would find him and somehow make sense of his life. He remembered the quiet voice during his injury. *"His love brings strength."*

He decided that it was time to think and pray.

Chapter 9

THE ROAD NORTH

27 AD
JERUSALEM

Just before dawn, Matthias stood outside the southern gate of the Temple. In the lightless solitude of the morning, Matthias could hear faint noises announcing that early preparations for the morning meal had begun in the Temple. Suddenly, the eight-foot wooden door started to open, stop, and then finally creak open to reveal a face. A voice whispered, "Matthias?"

"Is that you, Nicodemus?"

"Yes, old friend. Once again, you've agreed to serve our God."

"I never stopped, Nic. How are you, my friend? It is good to see you again. I hear you are becoming an important Pharisee in the Sanhedrin. Are you keeping the Council in check?"

"You know I can only make my voice heard; I can't make them listen. But I will never yield my faith. In the end, God prevails." Nicodemus chuckled. "I still pray for the day you will return from this pilgrimage of yours and rejoin the living, Matthias."

"Nic, you know better than I do that God has separate paths for each of us. God chose my path as a rabbi, then Zealot, and now this path as a merchant to help with underground connections. And with your blessing, if you remember."

"I remember, but I still miss my friend. Especially the days we studied in the Temple together. You have always done God's work. You were a good rabbi. Now, you do the work we cannot do in the open. Ironically, in many ways, Matthias, I envy your freedom and life. I seem so confined here in the Temple."

Matthias laughed. "You mean until the Romans or King Herod's guards catch up with me!"

"You're a brave and dedicated man, Matthias. Even as a Zealot, you looked after your followers. God will not forget your sacrifices."

"How is life in the Temple, my friend?" asked Matthias.

"Since Joseph Caiaphas has been appointed high priest by the Romans, it's been a political nightmare. Now he wants King Herod's throne and Pontius Pilate's control over Judea. All he thought about was being the next king while he was the High Priest of Judea. And he gets more ambitious each year."

Nicodemus frowned and handed Matthias a pouch, heavy with the payment for his trip. "May peace be with you, Matthias. I've also added some extra for Sabbath meals during your trip."

"Thank you and may peace be with you, Nic. Stay safe in your brood of vipers!" Matthias frowned as he walked away in the early morning sunlight of Jerusalem.

OLD FRIENDS, MUDDY ROADS

Matthias chose his traveling companions carefully. His 'herdsmen' to drive the animals back to Jerusalem also doubled as guards. They were close friends from his earlier Zealot days. As his men gathered in an old wooden warehouse near the walls of Jerusalem, Levi, Shulman, and Kantor were hitching up two carts to the donkeys.

In truth, Levi and Shulman were more than old friends—they were also hardened Zealot warriors with dozens of Roman skirmishes behind them. Along with Jonathan's father Joseph, they had stood side by side fighting against Roman soldiers in their youth.

The fourth was Shulman's son, Kantor, a gangly young man of twenty, young but trustworthy with an archer's bow. All had served Matthias well in previous cross-country excursions and numerous trade deals.

They came at Matthias's request, not for the wages but for the loyalty to a man who had given so much of himself. They came because of Joseph, Jonathan's father, a fallen compatriot to whom they owed so much from their youth. Kantor came because of adventure, and an opportunity for an experience outside of Jerusalem.

Matthias and his men also knew this trip north would be difficult. The spring of 27 AD was not particularly kind to the roads north, through Samaria and into Galilee. The winter had been dry but recent spring rains made the roads slick and muddy in Judea, then pitted and ruddy in Samaria. That morning, the temperature had dropped in Jerusalem. Each spoken breath brought a frosty cloud of mist.

After loading stores onto the carts, Matthias maneuvered his friends and wagons through the city's Fish Gate to the road north. Muddy roads slowed their progress, muddy sandals became heavy, and the donkeys' hooves needed frequent cleaning from embedded small rocks.

"Matthias! Could you have picked a colder day?" Schulman was shivering.

"Walk faster and you'll get warmer!" responded Matthias. Levi snickered and Kantor lowered his hood over his face.

"This could be a long trip," Schulman quipped.

"There will be warm drinks for everyone tonight," Matthias promised his friends.

By the second day, the weather had begun to clear, and the troupe had worked their way north, past the towns of Ephraim and Alexandrium. Each day Matthias sent Levi and Kantor ahead to visit the farms along the northern road leading out of Judea to determine the availability and price of sheep, cattle, doves, and wheat. Each time came the same answer: livestock was scarce, and prices were high.

Undaunted, Matthias pressed northward, watchful for roaming thieves and Roman patrols that might attack and rob them of their supplies and money for the trip. Matthias was driving his men quickly through Judea, trying hard not to be noticed. Stopping at night meant sleeping close to the cart and donkeys. After the first night, the troupe went without fires to warm them, keeping as silent and inconspicuous as possible. His goal was to get into Samaria quickly, where he and his cohort would be less likely to be known.

After three days of hard walking and cold nights, Matthias was relieved to arrive on the outskirts of Anata, a small town on the Samaria border. They were finally far from the marauding thieves that frequented the roads in northern Judea, and away from Roman patrols out of Alexandrium. Entering Anutan, there were sighs of relief and hopeful prayers for better markets and warmer days.

Matthias also appreciated the different landscape and climate of Samaria. Temperatures were more moderate, and winter was abating. Warm weather was just a few weeks away, and already they could see the budding leaves of the Cyprus and olive trees that covered the rolling hills. For a change, there was sufficient shade for rest stops and some small protection from the occasional spring rain shower. Small streams along the road provided them with water, lightening the load of needing to carry heavy sheepskin bags.

By the next evening, Matthias's cohort had reached the outskirts of the small town of Sychar. Resting outside the city in an olive grove, they celebrated with the warmth of an open fire and hot water for cooking. The next morning, Matthias entered Sychar, hopeful that he would be able to purchase a quantity of doves, guaranteed by deposits, with a final payment on their return trip to Jerusalem.

By the midafternoon, Matthias entered their camp. "Success! Praise be to our Lord. We've secured our first contract of the trip!"

The cohort cheered Matthias. "Great news master merchant! Are we rich?"

Then Levi quickly broke in. "But whom did you have to sell into bondage? Oh, please don't say it was Kantor . . . he's too young to be working as a goat herder's assistant!" Levi and Shulman laughed as Kantor grimaced.

"No Levi, I offered Kantor, but they refused! It's because he's too handsome. They were afraid he'd attract all the young maids in the town and no work would get done!" joked Matthias. "They asked for you!" This time everyone laughed, relieved that there was some small measure of success in their journey.

As usual, the cohort started before dawn the next day. But after another two days of walking through Samaria, stopping along the way to make small purchases of cattle and sheep, Matthias became concerned. He hoped that most of the animals could have been purchased in Samaria and, if needed, he would enter Galilee to complete his final purchases. But the winter in Samaria had proven hard on livestock. Only a few farmers were willing to part with their stock of sheep or cattle. The only thing they were not short of was migrating doves.

PRAYER OF THANKS

By the fifth day, it was late afternoon when Matthias directed the men up a steep hill through a pine grove. Atop the hill, the men could see beyond the trees into the Jezreel Valley. Matthias ordered a camp for the night, where they would rest on the Sabbath the next day.

Atop the hill, Matthias gazed for miles ahead, standing there quietly with his thoughts. Levi, Shulman, and Kantor realized they had entered Galilee and stood gaping at the valley ahead. Farm after farm in the Jezreel Valley seemed to blossom with life. Two hours later, the sun had set between the pine trees, providing the foursome a beautiful backdrop of crimson-red clouds for their Sabbath meal.

Matthias lit the Sabbath candles, held onto his prayer shawl, and recited from the Torah by heart. "Barukh atah Adonai, Eloheinu, melelch ha'olam." Matthias began with blessings over the candles. The men repeated the prayer in unison after Matthias, the man who had once been their temple rabbi, then their Zealot leader.

Resting on the Sabbath day lightened the spirits of the four travelers. Seeing the deep greenness of the Jezreel Valley gave them hope their journey north would be successful. It was early in the season, and new crops had already been planted. From the hilltop, the men could see numerous cattle and sheep covering large grasslands along the valley.

When the evening had quieted down, Kantor pulled his father aside and whispered. "Was Matthias really a rabbi in the Temple?"

"Yes, son, he was, a long time ago," responded Shulman.

"Why did he leave?" came the immediate question from Kantor.

"Matthias was an excellent rabbi, son. That's where we first met him, a young rabbi in the Temple. He would always take great care to explain the Torah to us in ways we could understand and relate to our daily lives. He talked to us plainly, we knew he cared about us. We also knew that he was frustrated and angry with how Rome treated us. He would talk about us ruling our own land and not being subjected to Roman rule."

"He also started to get into trouble with the Pharisees. He kept asking them why the temple taxes were so high and complaining that our people in Jerusalem were going hungry. But they just ignored him."

Shulman continued, "So, one day he took money from the Temple to buy Passover food for a destitute family who had recently lost their father. When the Pharisees found out what he had done, they were livid. They banished Matthias from the Temple rituals and teaching. Months later, with the help of a friend, a priest named Nicodemus, he was later restored to his teaching duties, but his heart was no longer with the Temple. He soon left and joined the Zealots to fight for the Jews' freedom from the Romans. It wasn't long before Levi and I joined him in that fight."

Shulman looked at his son and then back to the firepit where Matthias and Levi were warming their feet in the cool night air.

Kantor looked over to the fire and sighed, "You fought with him?"

"Yes son, and I would follow Matthias into the gates of hell if he asked. We followed him because there was honor in his actions. It made life worth living. We all have chances to live, but not every man has an opportunity to become alive," Schulman answered his son with a heavy sigh.

"It's time to get some sleep. We have a long journey ahead of us, son," Schulman finished.

Two days later, Matthias's cohort entered the city of Nain. Within days, they were able to acquire enough sheep and cattle, ensuring the success of the trip. Matthias stopped at sunset to offer prayers; his journey had turned a corner and their risk taken had turned into success. Livestock seemed to be abundant, and cattle and sheep prices were reasonable.

That night, Matthias secured lodging for the four men in a tavern, a welcome treat. In a large room upstairs, Matthias ordered a hot meal of roasted lamb, the first since their departure. Besides the lamb, the men enjoyed nuts, bread, dates, and wine to celebrate their success. There was only one thing remaining.

Midway through the dinner, Matthias stood to make an announcement. "I must travel alone a bit farther north tomorrow. Shulman, you oversee this pack of bandits until I get back."

"Who is she? I think it must be a long-lost sweetheart!" Levi bellowed, provoking more jests from Shulman and Kantor.

Laughing, Matthias replied, "If I were that young! No, I have a special errand to find some help for rebuilding the inn. We need carpenters. I've heard they have plenty in Galilee. This is the last requirement of this trip."

"Fine, Matthias, as long as she has hazel eyes!" said Levi. Laughing, the men started toasting Matthias's long-lost sweetheart and played a game of guessing the color of her eyes and hair.

YESHUA AND JAMES

"Are you all right, James?" Yeshua inquired. "You seem tired today, my brother. Take a rest."

James was sweating and looked drained. They had been cutting and carrying stone blocks to build a foundation for a new house. It was mid-day and the brothers had not taken a break since dawn.

"I don't want to rest while you work. Let's both take time for a break and a meal. The sun is draining our energy," James said.

Yeshua looked at James and nodded, "Good idea. Let's rest. We've worked hard today."

As Yeshua and James walked to a nearby cypress grove for shade, Yeshua looked up to see a man approaching, wearing plain clothes but walking with the confidence of one accustomed to authority. Yeshua set down the saw and hammer.

"James, I'll be right back. I'll join you after I talk to this man at the edge of the trees."

After a brief encounter, Yeshua returned to his brother.

"James, good news. We have a job in Jerusalem. It will give us a chance to work out of the sun for a while."

"That is good news!" James's mood brightened as he filled his cup from the leather water pouch.

"Jerusalem will be a nice break. We can see the Temple and purchase new tools."

"When do we go?" James asked.

"After we finish this job and celebrate Passover with Mom.

"The family we will work for needs our help. We will likely find more than just physical work in Jerusalem."

"Does that mean we will earn bottom wages again?"

"It means we will earn a fair wage," Yeshua smiled. "There is more to Jerusalem than just easier jobs."

Conflicting thoughts nagged Yeshua's consciousness. He enjoyed working in construction and carpentry, but he knew this part of his life was coming to an end. There was so much more to be done in this world. He knew the prophecies; he knew the things that had to be done for his Heavenly Father. Nonetheless, Yeshua looked forward to the break of working in Jerusalem for a while, to return to the Temple and study and debate with the rabbis again.

With each previous trip to Jerusalem, Yeshua's heart was uplifted. Although raised in Egypt and Nazareth, he was always drawn to Jerusalem, as though he was coming home.

Throughout his life, lessons from the Scriptures came naturally to him, as though he personally knew the history outlined in the Torah, even before reading them. Yeshua had found delight in his studies with the rabbis. His natural insights allowed him to put the pieces of God's puzzle together in ways that made sense, especially as he explained the Torah to others. Some said it was a gift from God.

Priests and rabbis worked hard to learn and understand the meanings of the Torah, but Yeshua simply understood. He knew the truths and stories of the Torah as though he had lived them. Yet his frequent probing questions created a disturbing ripple with the rabbis in the local Temple.

Yeshua realized that the expansion of God's laws by the Priests was not what their Father had wanted. He knew the inherent conflict between trying to keep an expanding set of rabbinical laws, as opposed to simply knowing and loving their God, would come to a dramatic confrontation someday.

"James, when in Jerusalem, I'd like to go to the Temple when I can. I have some studying to do in the library."

THE RETURN

"You've been working too hard, Jonathan; you can't continue at this pace," Matthias remarked. Jonathan's exhaustion was obvious. "And we have carpenters coming. I hired two men from Nazareth. Once they finish their construction work in Nazareth and celebrate Passover with their family, they will come here to help. They are highly recommended, and their price was reasonable. It is low for Jerusalem standards. I think the older carpenter wants to be a rabbi. I have a strong feeling we can trust them."

Jonathan laughed sarcastically. "After Jason, I trust your opinion more than mine, Matthias."

"I'm sorry that Jason didn't work out. Giving him an opportunity was no sin or folly. But you need to stop beating yourself up; you made no mistake. You felt like the kid deserved a chance and you gave him one. There's no shame in that."

"I think we can get back on track if these new men work out. I've been thinking during your trip. Let's work on finishing the tavern first, then the lodging. We can have the new carpenters work on the lodging downstairs and upstairs while we finish the kitchen and tavern area," suggested Jonathan.

"Not a bad idea. We should be able to make it work," Matthias replied.

SPRING IN JERUSALEM
28 AD

The late spring was hot in Judea. Jonathan understood the effects of these hot days on rebuilding the inn. Men often lagged in the heat.

On that morning, Jerusalem was filled with a cool mist, leading many to hope for a pleasant day without heat. But it was an illusion. By 10 in the morning, the heat had descended on the city, drying up any hope of a cooler summer day.

Despite the heat, these new carpenters from Nazareth seemed tireless in their work. As they labored, there was a calming effect to their efforts. They were diligent, not hurried, and they often took time to check their work before starting another task. It was during these interludes that Jonathan would find them smiling and jesting with each other as they worked in the heat. It was apparent they loved the effort of rebuilding the inn, as though every task was an opportunity to be creative. There was joy in their work. Jonathan watched and was amazed, yet somewhat skeptical that they may still have ulterior motives he had not yet discovered.

By the early fall, the construction was going well, ahead of schedule. Being around the Nazareth brothers brought a new sensation for Jonathan. With each encounter, Jonathan felt a growing sense of hope that allowed him to relax. He looked forward to the meals where they often laughed with each other. Jonathan found Yeshua's conversations fascinating. It wasn't long before he discovered Yeshua was a scholar, quoting sacred texts and discussing the logic behind the Torah. He also found out something else that was remarkable.

Jonathan learned that Yeshua often used his free time to discuss the Tanakh and especially the Torah with the rabbis and Pharisees in the temple, other times studying in the Temple library. Jonathan had even heard rumors that Yeshua, without formal training, understood the sacred Scriptures better than most Pharisees.

SARA

Daylight crept through the clouds in eastern Jerusalem when Sara started to prepare breakfast for Jonathan and Mara.

Jonathan typically staggered into the kitchen, grabbed a handful of bread, smattered on some butter and honey if available, then rushed out with a piece of fruit as though Romans were chasing him.

In truth, Sara knew fears were haunting her son. Jonathan was increasingly haunted by the fear of failure, giving in to the inner voices telling him that his efforts were going to end in disaster.

Sara could almost hear the doubts plaguing Jonathan. *You're not worthy, Jonathan. What makes you think you can turn this dilapidated building into a profitable inn?'*

Despite her best efforts to console him, Jonathan's response was one he had repeated in the past. "God abandoned us when father died."

Jonathan's retort cut through Sara's heart, magnifying her fears and loneliness. Leaving the room, she could only cry out and pray to a distant God, wondering why he had turned his back on his people. She knew the Jews had many times broken their covenant with their God, always to their pain and regret.

Yet remarkably the Jews continued the pattern. One generation would repent, another ignored their God, and the last would blatantly abandon Him. This time Sara feared her God had walked away from them for good. It had been over 400 years since a prophet had come to lead the Jews out of their misery.

Her fear of isolation from God exacerbated her mounting worries about her son. He was aging quickly beyond his youth, and she feared she could lose him, too.

Today, there would be extra mouths to feed again, so she prepared additional flatbread and figs. The carpenters from Nazareth never asked for breakfast, often claiming a lack of hunger. But Sara knew differently.

She had seen her husband too weak to work by mid-morning without breakfast. But that wasn't the true reason she continued to press breakfast into their hands and ignored their refusals. Each day that they worked on the inn, they brought their new home an increasing measure of peace. It wasn't just that their work was progressing well, or that the inn was starting to look like a real building—it was something she couldn't articulate yet. She found herself singing inside when they were present, almost as though they brought a wall of emotional refuge with them each day.

Puzzled, she found herself staring at Yeshua and James, inwardly finding small pieces of hope, outwardly smiling. When Yeshua or James looked in her direction, she immediately walked away as though she was just planning her next task.

Today, she would not let them refuse breakfast.

"You will come in and have some porridge, honey, and dates," Sara insisted. While this was not quite a command, both Yeshua and James knew the authoritative voice of a mother.

James answered, knowing Yeshua would have a problem accepting their meals out of a sense of love for this family. "You honor us. You have been kind to us throughout the work we have done here."

"Bless you, Sara. Your heart is full," added Yeshua. "Let us give thanks to God. He is indeed a wonderful God. You give when you have little, you love when you have a wounded heart, you serve when it is we who should honor you."

Sara stepped back and looked down. His words reached inside her and freed emotions from the bonds of her scars, each year becoming stronger as she relived the death of her husband and shed tears for her children.

She wondered how this man could see so deeply, how mere words could unleash the pain she had chained up inside her heart for all these years. She turned and fought back tears. His words touched too deeply. But she couldn't show her pain; it was not his burden to bear.

"It will be cold before you start to eat. Go outside and wash in the basin!" she ordered gruffly.

As James walked outside with Yeshua, he whispered to his brother, "Your words have touched Sara, perhaps too deeply."

"Yes, they have. She will have to trust God to become strong again and find joy in this life. She worries about Jonathan and Mara, as do I. Jonathan is a good man, but he bears a terrible burden. He thinks he let his father die. He still does not know who he is, he just knows that he must accomplish so much. My heart aches for him. He walks in daily fear of failure.

"Go inside, James. Sara needs someone in the room to distract her. Serving others is a place where she feels safe. Give her peace by receiving her gift. I will be in shortly. I need to pray."

Yeshua walked across the courtyard and found Jonathan finishing his hurried meal, preparing for the day. Jonathan looked up and saw the carpenter walk towards him, his eyes focused on Jonathan with intention.

Jonathan stiffened, preparing for the worst. He knew the work they performed was worth twice the wages he could afford to pay them.

"Jonathan, your mother has been so kind to us. I thank you for her service and the sacrifices of your family."

Jonathan relaxed a bit and looked up at Yeshua's penetrating eyes. "Your work has been more than I deserve, Yeshua. Both of you work as though you love the hard labor. You are building this inn as if it were the Temple. I wish I could thank you more, but you know we are struggling."

"James and I would not accept more from you. It has been our honor to resurrect this inn for you. As you know, we will be finishing after the new year. We would like to see your inn blessed by the rabbis. And you will need more help here, Jonathan. All three of you work too hard, especially on the Sabbath."

Jonathan slowly responded, "The rabbis and Pharisees abandoned my family when my father died. Asking them to bless this inn would dishonor the memory of my father, and frankly, I cannot afford their 'honorary' gift anyway." He continued, "As for additional help, I agree with you. But again, whom can I afford?"

"Yes, I know," Yeshua replied. "But sometimes the gifts God offers are hidden in the pain of the past. If you would allow me, I would like to bless this inn when it is restored. There is no gift necessary for a simple carpenter. Your kindness has been a gift to us. But there is a solution to finding more help. There is a man in debtors' prison whom you could free for the price of his service, to work off the debt he owes this family. At least until the debt is paid, his service would be the cost of his lodging."

Jonathan was taken aback. He hadn't thought about Jason for quite a while. How could he forgive him? Bringing Jason back would show weakness, frailty. Jonathan just managed to mutter, "What did you say?"

"The strongest thing you could do now is to trust . . . trust God. Your heart is good. But you need to take that next step and forgive. Pray to our Heavenly Father, soften your heart, and He will hear you. Forgive and you can be released from your pain and the weight you bear. We all need His help."

Jonathan stuttered, "I can—I can do this myself, Yeshua. I don't need Jason. He stole from me. He threatened our lives with his drunken greed!"

"You need to forgive Jason. A rescued man can be more loyal and a greater servant than you can ever imagine. Forgive Jason, as our Father has forgiven the Jews for their sins so many times. Hope is never lost. Pray. Forgiving will set you free. You are stronger than you think."

Yeshua held Jonathan's gaze. He saw the pain in his eyes, he saw the love in his eyes. He cried out again. "He stole from me! I saw my father die. I held his head as God watched him die. My father! How can I forgive, Yeshua? How do I stop the hurt in my life?"

"No, Jonathan, God was with you the day the Roman soldier drew out his knife in defense. The soldier did not mean to kill. But God was with both of you," Yeshua said gently. "He was with you when you were chased by Barabbas the thief. He was with you the day you met Matthias. He was with you when Matthias was stabbed. It was God who saved him. He saved him for you, Jonathan. And he was with you the day after when you cried out asking God why this was happening to you. He is with you now. Don't let go of his love, Jonathan."

"How did you know that? I've never talked to anyone about those things?"

Perplexed, Jonathan was on the verge of breaking down. Garnering his strength, he struggled to rally his confidence and pride.

"I don't need to discuss this with you today." Jonathan turned and wiped his eyes as he walked away.

Chapter 10

COURAGE TO FORGIVE

28 AD

JERUSALEM

JONATHAN

It took several hours before Jonathan calmed down enough to seriously consider Yeshua's words, which kept repeating in his head. *"Don't let go of his love."*

'Pray? Forgive so that I can be free? How did he know those things about Matthias?'

Jonathan ran through the streets of Jerusalem, turned a corner at an old wooden storehouse, directly into the crowded marketplace. But something was wrong. Everyone was standing, no one moving. Vendors and customers stared at a corner of the market where two men appeared to be fighting.

As Jonathan looked closer, what he saw infuriated him. A Roman soldier stood above an old man, beating him for not carrying the soldier's armor and sacks past the obligatory mile allowed by Roman law. As Jonathan stared at the Roman soldier, his anger turned to fury. He stepped back around the corner. He knew the law; the Roman had a legal right to have a Jew carry his burden, but for only a mile.

Kneeling, Jonathan began to pray, holding his hands over his face to hide his tears.

"Oh God, how can this happen? How can we be slaves in our own land? Lord my God, save that man. Save us, Lord. Forgive me of my sins, Lord. Am I as arrogant as that soldier?"

Jonathan knelt quietly for several minutes. The wind began to rustle, and he thought he heard a whisper echoing in the wind. "*Forgive him.*"

Shaking his head, Jonathan stood up and turned the corner again. What he saw stopped him in his tracks. Jonathan stood frozen at the corner of the building, watching a much larger Roman soldier grab the first soldier by the breastplate and throw him against the stone wall of a nearby building. The hapless Jew ran down the street, away from the soldiers.

Looking a second time, Jonathan recognized the second soldier. He was the same Roman Standard from the night he and Matthias had been attacked by the thieves. The same Roman officer that had saved their lives.

"Report back to the fortress, Tavian. You've gone too far, again. I'll deal with you when I get back. If you disobey my orders, I'll have you flogged!"

The Roman officer looked around at the surrounding crowd of merchants and customers. Before his eyes found him, Jonathan quickly ducked around the corner. Moving quickly down the adjacent street, Jonathan shook his head in wonder and thanked God for this small measure of justice.

'How could this be a coincidence? Did God just answer my prayer?'

Jonathan knew what he needed to do next. He turned another corner, passing through another market. As he increased his pace to a jog, he couldn't help but bump into market customers getting through the crowded street. After a year with barely a thought of Jason, Jonathan was now determined to get him out of the debtor's prison. There was no time to waste.

JASON

The Roman prison was beyond filthy. Prisoners suffered daily with the rats and the stench of decaying bodies. Jason was no exception. His cell was crowded with eleven other lice-infested, wretched prisoners barely sustained on water and gruel. A bath was a monthly dousing with a bucket of water by another inmate.

Daily, Jason fought to survive, often one moment at a time, taking each morning as a victory over the previous day.

During his first month in the prison, Jason suffered convulsions, vomiting, hallucinations, and seizures of alcohol withdrawal. Since then, malnutrition and hard labor had worn Jason to almost a skeleton. Barely surviving on meals that wouldn't sustain a dog, Jason hung onto a belief that his salvation was still possible.

Then after months of hoping and praying, Jason's understanding of his situation became clear. He would not live long enough to pay off his debt. Yet there was no other goal—just survival for one more day. Hard days of labor coupled with beatings to force the inmates to work even harder produced horrific nights. He lay in his blackened stone cell, shivering, fighting off biting rats with bleeding fingers.

During those nights, Jason often prayed for a merciful death. He prayed to a God he had never known, cursing the demons that captured his soul with the ropes of his drunkenness. Jason often screamed at the realization he had sold his soul for a bottle of wine, never considering the consequences. Yet he continued to pray to a God he feared had forgotten him; it was the only thing he could do.

From the corner of the cell came a shrieking voice, "You think your God is listening, you damn fool?" barked Gestas. Caught by Roman soldiers trying to rob two beggars in an alley over a year ago, Gestas was a seasoned veteran of Cell VII. "At least on the streets, we knew who our God was. No matter what you did, no matter who you were, our master was gold and silver. I will get out of this sh*t hole as soon as my friends settle matters with that bastard Roman officer."

Jason just looked down and avoided Gestas's gaze, which signaled another burst of anger from the prisoner.

"Hold onto those prayers and don't let go, drunkard. It will be your surviving grace," laughed Gestas.

Jason just turned his head, too broken to cry, too alone to fight.

After his first three months in the Roman prison, Jason found his God in the darkness of another sleepless night. Trembling and sweating, he prayed the words of a broken man. Sober and completely conscious of the wreck his life had become, he prayed that he might have a purpose in God's world. He prayed and waited for God's answer. For the next year, praying kept the darkness at bay from Jason. It kept him alive.

Then one day a guard approached his cell and called out in a gruff voice that held no emotion other than contempt. "Jason! Are you still alive, you thieving bastard?"

Jason fought the urge to respond but remained quiet. Guards never looked for prisoners except to delight in some sadistic torture.

"Jason are you alive today?" laughed the guard.

He muttered, "Jason died last week."

The guard laughed again, "That's too bad. We were going to put him on a golden pedestal and anoint him the new prison prophet. Where is his body, you prison lice?"

It was Gestas who answered. "He's hiding in the corner like a prison rat! Go have fun with him. We won't have to hear his prayers anymore."

The guard opened the cell door and stepped inside. "Throw him outside or there won't be a supper for anyone tonight, you bastards!"

There was a rumbling, muffled screams, and Jason was hurled outside the cell. Over a year inside the prison had left him emaciated beyond recognition. His hair was blacked from mud and lice. He wore the face of a hollow man, sunken cheeks and eyes betraying his last few days of life. He looked more like a skeleton wrapped in skin, than a man. He lay outside the cell as the guard laughed at him. Jason doubted he could even stand up.

With an effort beyond his understanding, he shifted forward and used a bony elbow to leverage himself onto both knees.

"This is your lucky day, Jason. Your debt has been forgiven; you are free to go."

Jason heard the guard's words but could not believe them.

"Get up, you mangy bastard!" cried the guard. "Or we'll tell the merchant you are dead."

Jason shook his head. '*God answered me. God answered my prayer.*'

"I'm alive," were the only words he could manage. "I'm alive!" Grunting and crying with the pain, Jason stood. He started moving forward, one painful step at a time.

Jonathan stood outside the prison, waiting for the guards to release Jason. When a guard told him to be prepared for a sick man, he thought Jason might be ill from dysentery. But when Jason appeared, Jonathan couldn't believe it was him— there was nothing recognizable about the skeleton standing before him. Shaken by the realization of the pain he had imposed upon this man, Jonathan asked, "Jason, is this you?"

Tears ran down Jason's muddied cheeks. It was as though pain ran through every nerve in his body, climbing its way to his eyes and running down his limbs. Jason was frozen in place. But then he nodded and raised a hand toward Jonathan. A minute passed with the two men staring at each other.

Eventually, Jason muttered, "Jonathan. I am sorry."

Jonathan fought back his tears. '*What have I done?*' "Can you walk, Jason?" he whispered. "I'm taking you home. You need to rest and eat first. We'll talk later after you have cleaned yourself and had time to heal."

Jason stood, his bloodshot eyes fixated upon Jonathan, tears flowing down his matted beard, dangling like liquid crystals. "I'm so sorry, Jonathan," Jason repeated, the only words he could manage as he dropped to his knees, his hand reaching out to Jonathan.

Jonathan grabbed his hand and stood motionless, dumbfounded. He understood what Yeshua meant now. Jonathan was now the indebted one, standing inside a memory he could never forget. He gently pulled Jason up, wrapped his arm around him and led him to his new home, back to the inn.

JONATHAN

Back at the inn, Jonathan's mind was twisting. Who was this man, Yeshua, and how could he be just a carpenter? *'This carpenter knew my mind, as though he could hear my fears, my anger.'*

How could he tell anyone about the voices he heard? They would think he was exhausted or hallucinating. He felt alone, unsure. Could he confide in Sara or Mara? Matthias would lose trust in him. How could he turn their world up-side-down when so much depended upon him?

His only choice was to keep silent. But shadows of fear continued to dance in Jonathan's mind. Now he was also responsible for Jason. The man needed rest and nourishment.

Jonathan entered the kitchen and found Susanna and his mother preparing the evening meal. "Susanna, I need your help. Can you find that young physician who helped Matthias? We need his help to save someone I've brought back to the inn."

The next day Luke arrived to examine Jason. His report was not encouraging.

"I won't lie to you. He's near death. We've shaved his head and beard to get rid of the lice. But his emaciated body will take months to recover, there's a lot of damage inside his organs." Luke's face did not hide his concern. "You're a decent man to rescue him from prison, Jonathan."

The comment pained Jonathan. "No, Luke, I'm not. I put him there for stealing. I'm not proud of what I did. I didn't know how they would treat him; I didn't really care or think about it. I was so angry." Looking down, Jonathan whispered, "Now I'm ashamed."

Luke lowered his head and spoke softly. "He's so thankful that you saved his life. Odd that he doesn't seem to bare any malice. He knows his own decisions created his pain. He keeps saying you gave him hope. It seems that it's time to forgive yourself, Jonathan."

Jonathan just nodded. He wasn't sure. How could he ever pretend to be a better man? His mind continued to get lost in the woods. And there were demons in the woods that would steal his spirit while fueling his fears, anger, and pride. Jonathan felt as though his soul was at war with itself and he was losing the battle.

WORKING ON THE INN

"Brother, she's staring at us again," whispered James.

"I know. Sara enjoys seeing us work," replied Yeshua.

"But it seems odd. Please talk to her."

"I will for you," Yeshua chuckled. "I will talk with her. But it is hard to fault a smiling woman, particularly in this house. There have been many hardships here that even the fire that burned this place could not hide. I have been praying that our Lord would cast out the bad memories from this house. But they are firmly rooted here."

"I can feel them, too," James said. "Please pray harder. I know God listens to you."

CASSIUS

The fall brought a rare respite in the palace from normal work. King Herod had taken a trip to Galilee with his family. After a thorough cleaning of the palace, Chuza declared a day off for the servants. Immediately, Joanna and Mary marshaled a plan for Mary to gather food from the kitchens while Joanna got word to Cassius to meet them in the gardens, just outside the eastern gate of Jerusalem. For a day, they were free.

An hour later, Cassius walked through the Gardens of Gethsemane looking for Mary and Joanna. To his surprise, Mary was waiting for him with a lunch basket. As Cassius approached, Joanna rose and smiled at him.

"I have business back at the palace, Cassius. Can you make sure Mary is safe in her return?"

"You have my word, Joanna." Cassius smiled as he sat on the grass next to Mary.

For months Mary had been secretly meeting with Cassius in the palace. With each encounter, they had grown to understand each other more. Cautious not to be seen by either palace servants or guards, they kept their encounters brief, leaving them desperate for their next visit. After the first month, Cassius became curious about Mary's background and asked her to teach him more about the Jews and their history. Soon their meetings had a purpose, Mary teaching him about her world and Cassius responding with stories about his youth in Tuscany.

"My mother was Jewish," said Cassius, "but she rarely talked about her religion in the house. I think out of respect for my father. You tell me that your God gave this land to the Jews over 1,200 years ago? And it was Joshua, not Moses, who led the Jews into this land? Why did your God not let Moses into the new land?" Cassius gave Mary a quizzical look as he tore the bread and cut some goat cheese for their lunch.

Mary laughed, "God loved Moses very much, but Moses allowed his people to disobey God's command to enter Canaan and take the land. So, God banished the Jews back into the desert for 40 years. God would not let Moses enter the land because he had also disobeyed God. Then God commanded Joshua to enter Canaan and take the land that God had promised. And Joshua did it."

"It sounds like your God can get angry at you Jews?"

"Yes, he can." Mary sighed. "That's because our God has saved our people from destruction so many times and made covenants with us for our protection. He just asks that we obey and worship only Him. But we can be a very stubborn people."

"Oh, I don't think I can respond to that. If I agree, you'll assault me with grapes, and we'd lose our lunch fruit. If I

disagree, you'll know I'm lying and won't trust me again."
Cassius laughed as he dodged a grape flying at his head.

"You underestimate me. I can still attack and have grapes
for lunch!"

As Cassius ducked away, he rolled on the blanket and
into Mary, holding onto her arm to steady himself. Mary
laughed as she collapsed onto the grass beneath the cypress
tree and lay beside Cassius. A long silence ensued as they
stared at each other, slowly closing the gap between them.

"It's time for more Aramaic lessons." Mary smiled as
Cassius shook his head to clear the pleasant fog growing in
his mind. "Your mother may have taught you the basics, but
you need practice!"

CALL TO DUTY

After returning to the fortress, Cassius was still daydreaming
about the day with Mary, alone in the garden. His thoughts
were interrupted when Centurion Orestes approached.

"Cassius, Tribune Valens wants to see you. Meet him in
his office at noon," directed the centurion.

Had he been seen with Mary? A jolt of fear shot through
him. He might be reassigned as a result, or worse, transferred
to a new post outside of Jerusalem. "Amicus, can you tell me
what the Tribune needs?" asked Cassius.

"No, but I know that Tribune Valens is getting tired.
The pressure of leading the Legion with the constant Zealot's
threats and harassment has worn on him."

"Yes sir, I've seen the same. I've worried about the pressures on him, particularly with Prefect Ambivulus's return to Rome. They were close."

"After more than ten years in Judea, Valens wants to see home again, especially his farm in northern Italy. Last month he confessed he misses the change of seasons there, the awakening of the trees, the singing of birds. I could tell that he is really homesick. Just be ready for new assignments, Cassius, you'll need to be flexible."

His comment worried Cassius even more. Mary was becoming an integral part of his life, digging deep ties into his heart. The thought of being reassigned outside of Jerusalem and leaving her did not just frighten him—it terrified him.

Cassius knocked on the wooden office door. Tribune Valens waved Cassius inside.

"I'm going home next month, Cassius. It's been planned for six months. I've written to the general of the garrison in Rome. I've talked to Pontius Pilate and King Herod. They all agree I may return home once a replacement has been nominated and trained. It's been over ten years since I've seen the wheat fields of my home."

Valens continued before Cassius could respond, "My replacement is named, and we'll start turning over my responsibilities to him as of tomorrow. You've served us well, Cassius. More than that, everyone feels comfortable about me retiring with you and Orestes here."

Valens chuckled, "You've come far since the days you rustled in the mud with your friend. Your military and leadership skills have continued to impress many in the Legion."

"Sir, but you've been our backbone for so long. How can we run the Legion without your leadership?"

Valens ignored his question. "I also understand you've acquired some Aramaic to speak directly with the Jews."

"Yes sir, but I'm not very good at it. My Greek is better." Cassius wasn't ready for a change of leadership.

"I could always trust your judgment, Cassius. You were right about the Zealots; they are becoming more emboldened. Their raids have caught the attention of the Senate. We'll need strong leadership to keep the rebels at bay."

"Sir, I will serve your replacement with the same effort, in your honor."

"That's good. Because my replacement is your Centurion, Orestes. And by the way, you are being promoted to fill his slot. Congratulations, you're the new Senior Centurion of the Xth Legion."

"But, sir, there are many more senior men in the Legion than I." Baffled, Cassius took a step back. He stared at Valens, not believing this was happening.

MARY AND CASSIUS

News spread quickly regarding Cassius's promotion. Mary had also heard the rumors in Herod's palace and was apprehensive of how this would affect their growing relationship. She'd never met anyone who would sit and listen to her for hours, wanting to know the details of her past and her dreams, wanting to be a part of her world. Mary was naturally apprehensive about losing their relationship—even so, she wasn't quite sure it was real. Cassius had become more than a friend and protector. For the first time since her parents had died, she felt safe. And she had grown to truly appreciate this man who had reached into her heart and touched her.

Cassius himself was stunned. Mary's affection was real, he was sure about that. Mary was all he wanted in his life. The promotion to Senior Centurion was unexpected, and in some ways unwanted. He had thought his position in life was set. He was comfortable being a standard in the Roman legions. He had responsibilities that he could easily accomplish; he was comfortable with his soldiers and his routine. But this promotion meant more than additional responsibilities. His routine and life were about to be dramatically altered. Mary might not understand that he would be unable to spend as much time with her as he wanted.

And then there was a nagging fear. If their relationship was discovered, they were both in for trouble. Mary might be flogged. Cassius could be demoted to a foot soldier for his relationship with one of Herod's slaves and sent abroad to another legion.

But there was also no question about refusing the promotion. First and foremost, Tribune Valens was a good man. Cassius valued his leadership and sense of justice. He knew Silus Valens cared deeply for the men in his command. He could not let down the man who had helped him ever since he came to the Xth Legion in Judea.

Entering the palace, Cassius turned a corner down the hallway toward the kitchens and servants' quarters, his head down to keep the outward world from invading his thoughts when Mary approached.

"Centurion Cassius!" she cried out before he ran into her.

Startled, Cassius looked up and became the fumbling soldier he had been on the day they had first met. "Mary!" Cassius called her name as a plea for help.

Mary whispered, "Can we talk tonight, outside the gates?"

Cassius looked around and simply nodded. Mary continued, "After the evening meals and cleaning. Nine o'clock outside the west gate."

OUTSIDE JERUSALEM

The moon was uncomfortably bright that night, it hung in the sky like a bright candle with a thousand starlit eyes peering behind it. It was bright enough that Cassius could clearly see Mary as she approached him through the western gate of Jerusalem.

Her head was covered with a shawl, her face indistinguishable in the darkness. But Cassius knew it was Mary. His heart started to race as he thought about the changes in their lives. Would she wait for him, knowing there might be weeks before they could see each other? Where was their relationship going? How could he free Mary from her servitude in Herod's household? Was he asking too much?

Cassius was wearing the plain tunic of a common merchant over his roman leather vest and uniform; his centurion helmet had been exchanged for a simple hood. He carried a six-foot walking stick, mostly to help his disguise but also for a bit of protection. Cassius made his best attempts to slouch, dropping his shoulders and leaning against the tree as though he was resting. At a distance, he was just a plain merchant or farmer, outside the gates of Jerusalem.

Seeing Mary approaching, he stepped outside the protection of the overgrown oak tree and peeled back his hood. Hesitantly, Mary walked past him toward the oak tree. Cassius waited a few moments to observe the night and then circled back toward the tree to join her. Mary surprised Cassius when she flung herself into his arms, holding him as though he was going on a long journey.

"I don't want to lose my friend, Cassius." Mary's eyes filled with tears. She looked up and saw the same fears in Cassius and held on even tighter.

"We won't let that happen. You are too important to me to let anyone stop what we have. You don't need to fear, Mary. We'll find a way. Pray to your God, Mary. I will pray to my gods as well."

The conversation lingered on for two hours, but it seemed as though it had just begun to Cassius. He looked up into the stars and moon and realized it was late and that Mary could be missed in the palace. He lowered his head and gently kissed her forehead. Mary held his hand and kissed it, holding her cheek in his palm.

"Mary, it is time to go. You must leave now, or you'll be missed, and we won't have any options for the future."

Mary hesitated, knowing Cassius was right. Pulling the shawl over her head again, she scuttled back toward the gate, followed by Cassius's eyes until he could see she was within the walls of Jerusalem.

Cassius sighed and then smiled. '*What are the gods up to now?*' he thought. Consciously he started back toward the gate, wanting to follow Mary, but not too closely. But close enough to hear if she was in trouble and could quickly intervene. He smiled after breathing in the remaining aroma her hair left on his tunic. It was a good sign, he thought.

Chapter 11

WE AREN'T THE SAME ANYMORE

29 AD

JERUSALEM

For six months, Mary and Cassius's relationship continued in secret. By the time spring came, they had formed a plan. If they could save 30 silver shekels, they could free Mary from her bondage. Cassius had been frugal. He didn't have any purpose for spending his wages. With his unspent savings, he hoped to purchase Mary's bondage. So far, he had collected 29 silver shekels.

Inadvertently, Mary was helping. Her seizures had increased over the past year. Even Herod had noticed and many in the palace were more concerned than ever that she was demon-possessed. She continued to keep herself disheveled to maintain her odd appearance.

But Mary was worried. Something was amiss. She could tell that friends and soldiers in the palace were talking. Every time she walked into a room; the conversation suddenly changed. Her secret relationship with Cassius was not so much of a secret to those she worked with. Cassius could be more discreet, tying his visits to inspecting the guards and security discussions with Herod, but it was different for Mary. She was a palace servant with few freedoms. Any discussion with Cassius in the halls of the palace was observed and noted.

Finally, Mary slipped Cassius a note during a brief passing as she was on her way to serve Herod's evening meal. Cassius turned the corner into Herod's gardens and stepped aside to read the note as Mary continued with her tray of fruit and meats. He grimaced, understanding the truth of her words.

Cassius, my love is growing for you daily, but we must be on guard to protect our secret. Meet me outside Jerusalem's walls, two miles past the Serpent's Pool on the road to Bethlehem, after the start of the second watch tomorrow night.

Cassius lowered his head. Their lives would easily spin out of control unless he acted soon.

Catching a glimpse of Mary as she departed the gardens, Cassius simply nodded his agreement. She gave him a quick smile and hurried back to the kitchens.

The next evening was chilly for late spring. It was convenient for Mary, as she could wrap herself in double layers of tunics, headdress, and veil covering her face against the western winds. The smell of rain permeated the air as she walked the two miles past the Serpent's Pool.

Stopping by a grove of trees, she spotted her tall, muscular man, again wearing a common tunic and cloak over his uniform. Although the clothes did not give Cassius away immediately, this time it was the Andalusian horse standing next to him. Venti revealed that he was not a common merchant. Mary had also become acutely aware of how different a Roman officer stood compared to common soldiers or merchants. As she walked closer to him, she smiled.

"Even now we are taking a risk, Mary. In two days, I'm going to approach Herod and buy your freedom. I've got the remaining shekels we need, plus a few for savings and buying a place to live," announced Cassius. "Will you become my wife?"

Mary turned away to hide her fears. Hope had taunted her over the years, always to be dashed by the reality that she was a bonded servant, little more than a slave in the palace of Herod Antipas. Her fear now overwhelmed her. '*Can this be real? I'm not an acceptable wife for a centurion.*'

When Mary turned back to face Cassius, tears flowed freely down her cheeks onto her cloak. "Tell me, Cassius. Tell me what you see. Tell me how you feel. Can you love a Jew, a woman who has fainting spells? The priests say I have demons, that I'm unworthy."

"From the moment I first saw you, Mary, I have loved you."

Cassius stepped back. Mary's questions brought uncertainty into his mind. He wondered if Mary could ever love a Roman soldier. "Mary, in your heart, can you love me?"

"Yes, with all my heart, Cassius," Mary replied.

Now his mind was made up. "Then I promise you, in two days you will be a free woman. In three days, we'll find a priest to marry us. We can be free from hiding our love."

"Yes, Cassius." Mary started to cry again, but this time she was smiling. For the first time in her life, she would be living with someone she chose, someone she loved and who loved her. Over the course of the past year, she had seen Cassius soften. His granite façade had developed cracks of kindness, a caring that ran deep into his soul. Mary saw standing before her a good man who would die protecting those he loved.

After an hour of talking about preparations for living in a home together, Mary was shaken by the reality that she could be a mother soon. The responsibility of having children brought both joy and fear to her heart. Was she ready?

"Mary, we need to go. We'll meet again in two days. After I've spoken to Herod, I'll come and get you. You'll be free."

Mary's heart was racing just thinking about the changes to come. She quickly turned, kissed Cassius's hand, and started back toward the palace.

CASSIUS

In the dim light of a quarter moon, Cassius watched as Mary began walking back to Jerusalem. Conscious that they could not be seen together, he stood there admiring her grace as she passed out of his sight. Cassius waited a few more minutes under the moonlit shadow of the oak tree, ensuring there was time enough for Mary to gain a good lead ahead of him. He would travel much faster on Venti. He took in the musky aroma of the ancient oak tree, then looked up at the tree that stood as a landmark alongside Bethlehem Road.

With Mary well out of sight, Cassius walked Venti back to the city walls of Jerusalem. With each step, Venti announced their presence by the clopping of his hooves on the cobbled road.

"What am I getting into, Venti? Every time I am with Mary, I don't feel the same. I'm a different person with her."

Venti lowered his head and snorted.

"We'll always be together, Venti. You won't lose me, you gain Mary," Cassius consoled his equine companion.

Venti turned his head and nudged Cassius, then whinnied.

"Hey, you have no complaints! I've seen you eyeing the mares in the fortress!" Cassius laughed as Venti started to prance.

"Settle down boy, we'll get you home soon enough to your ladies," Cassius smiled.

Finally, passing the Serpent's Pool outside the walls of Jerusalem, Cassius relaxed, feeling reassured that Mary was safe within the walls of the city. Then a dried tree limb snapped in the olive grove behind him. Curious, Cassius turned to walk back along the road. He wanted to make sure no one was following him or Mary. But he saw no one, so he continued walking on the road to Jericho.

Cassius turned to his horse, "I need to think this through, Venti. So many changes are happening right now."

Venti looked at Cassius and snorted again.

"You just have to worry about who feeds you," Cassius replied.

Venti nudged Cassius again, this time pushing him nearly off the road. "Okay, okay. Maybe you have a few other worries. But none like this." Cassius chuckled and continued to walk south. He needed time to think. He had proposed to Mary—he would be a husband soon. And then the promotion to Centurion and his new responsibilities. It might not be long before he became a father. A father?

"I guess we'll have to start a farm after this, Venti." He smiled and watched as the magnificent horse walked beside him, head up, and then out of nowhere, Venti started bucking on the road. Cassius assumed Venti was not particularly happy, they were not heading back to the stables and his hay.

In the woods ahead of them, a whispered voice was covered by the noise of Venti's hoofbeats.

"He's coming back, Barabbas," whispered Dismas.

"I see him. Quiet!" Barabbas was thinking through this opportunity. Overtaking the larger man would require coordination. In addition to his stature, Barabbas noted he walked with the authority of someone who had been in command. That meant he likely had hidden treasures under those tunics and probably had lost the strength he'd once had when he didn't have others to do his labors. If nothing else, there could be a ransom for his return. But they had four men, and the man with the horse was only one.

"Wait until he passes. Dismas, you've got the innocent face. You move down the road and then turn to face him in front of those oak trees. When he stops, ask him how far it is to the Jerusalem gates. We'll ambush him from all sides. Cestas, Ananias, cross the road and hide on the other side. When I raise my arm, move in to take him."

Dismas eagerly ran through the woods toward Bethlehem. After fifty yards, he stepped back onto the road and started walking toward Cassius as the others positioned themselves for the ambush.

Barabbas was sweating. He was desperate. Since the Roman patrols had hunted them in the city, the country had provided few rewards for a robber. He needed to prove to his men he could lead them to an easier life. So far, their efforts had not paid off.

Dismas slowly approached Cassius, but he did not look up. He stared down at the road, looking like a man who had more questions than answers.

"Good evening, stranger," Dismas said to Cassius. "Can you tell me how far the walls of Jerusalem are from here?"

It took a moment for Cassius to respond, startled because he did not notice the man on the road. "Yes, it's just a mile and a half to the center of the city walls," answered Cassius. A movement to his right caught his eye, but Dismas quickly engaged Cassius again.

"I'm a blacksmith looking for work. Do you know a place I could—" Dismas didn't have to finish. Cestas clubbed Cassius across the back of his head.

"No!" Cassius screamed. Dazed and stumbling from the blow, he released Venti, who pulled back and bolted down the road toward Jerusalem. Cassius reached out to strike an attacker with his left hand while he fumbled to grab the dagger hidden in his clothes.

Barabbas realized Cassius was a formidable foe and quickly delivered another blow across the head with his club. Cassius staggered, then fell to the ground.

Lying there, Cestas and Ananias stripped Cassius of his tunic and untangled him from his other clothes. Watching, Barabbas quickly discovered he was no merchant or palace manager. He was a Roman soldier. Even worse, his leather breastplate and dagger were worthy of an officer. Worse still, their victim wore a centurion's ring. Suddenly Barabbas realized he had seen this Roman before. It was during the fight with Jonathan and Matthias.

Barabbas knew the risk of robbing a merchant, but it was dangerous to rouse the might and fury of the Roman Legion in Jerusalem by attacking one of their senior officers.

"He's a Roman centurion! We've gone too far to stop. Strip him of his clothes!" ordered Barabbas. "Take his purse, tunic, cloak, and sandals. Give me his uniform."

"Leave him beside the road?" questioned Dismas. "But he could die."

"He's not moving. He might already be dead, and we'll be hunted by the Legion. Quickly!" demanded Barabbas. "We need to get off this road now. Move!"

Barabbas stared down at Cassius and noted that the centurion had been circumcised. He thought it odd for a Roman but knew this might help them escape. Passing-by travelers finding the body would believe he was a Jew. This could be their saving grace and give them time to hide in Jerusalem. They dragged Cassius to the edge of the road and then ran into the woods toward the city.

Cassius lay there through the night, bleeding from the side and back of his head. One of Barabbas's men had kicked him and broken a rib in the brief melee. Cassius drifted in and out of consciousness, balanced on a narrow causeway between life and death.

Shivering from the cold dampness, Cassius moaned and regained a foothold of consciousness. Yet he felt death was still coming. He prayed for Mary. '*May the gods keep her safe and find her someone who loves her as I did.*'

He wept as he prayed to meet his lost brother, Bracus, in Elysium. At least he would see him soon. Then he fell back into the void.

Somewhere during the morning, between small glimpses of consciousness, Cassius thought he saw the shadow of a man approach and kneel beside him. The stranger put his hand on Cassius, smiled, and whispered words Cassius couldn't hear. As He gently pressed his hand upon Cassius, an odd sensation of peace and relief swept through his broken body. The shadow stroked Cassius's blood-soaked hair. As quickly as he came, the stranger was gone. Again, Cassius was alone.

MORNING

Prostrate beside the Jericho Road, Cassius lay unconscious as merchants passed him by all morning. Naked, bloodied, and bruised, he lay in the field next to the road.

As they passed, many saw him. Some wanted to help but rationalized that the cost of trying to save him was too much.

A priest approached and thought. *'If I help him, then I'm responsible. It would take away from my Temple duties. My life is already full enough of other demands.'* And he walked away.

Others felt sorry for the naked merchant and thanked God it wasn't them. A Levite hurried by, looking straight ahead. Others just kept talking to each other as though they hadn't seen the wounded man.

It was mid-morning before a man from the north stopped and looked at Cassius. His eyes filled with tears as he remembered how he had been beaten and robbed just like this poor man. Samuel was a Samaritan, and he understood the risks of being an outcast. He knew the pain of broken ribs and shattered dreams. He quickly cleared his eyes and asked his servant to help him lift the man.

"Help me put him on my cart," Samuel muttered to Judas.

"Sire, we are just a few miles from the city gates. Certainly, someone else will find this wretch and help him. That is, if he's not dead already."

Samuel walked over to Cassius with a blanket. "At least this man deserves a blanket, even if he is dead."

Samuel started to cover the body, turning Cassius onto his side to secure the blanket. Then Cassius moaned.

Samuel shouted, "Quickly, he's alive. Help me bandage his wounds and lift him onto the cart."

'God has plans for this man,' thought Samuel.

He finished covering Cassius with a blanket and his tunic, then washed his head wounds the best he could with the water he carried in his sheepskin bag. After securing Cassius on the cart, Judas gave a whip to their donkey to get it moving, despite the extra load. They traveled toward Jerusalem.

"I know someone in Jerusalem who has an inn and could use some business," Samuel said. "He's a decent man who will understand the need for second chances."

When the cart rounded the bend to Jerusalem, it hit a rut in the road and jerked Cassius in the cart. Cassius moaned, "Mary."

It was another hour before they entered the gates of Jerusalem. Samuel turned and asked, "Judas, if this were me, would you have saved me from that ditch?"

"Of course, sire."

Facing the city walls, Samuel grimaced and thought, '*You were never a good liar, Judas.*'

Samuel recalled the time a man had saved him after a robbery and beating just outside the gates of Jerusalem, on the same road to Bethlehem. The stranger took him into his small house and nursed his wounds until Samuel was well enough to travel home to his wife and daughters. He was a carpenter who worked in Jerusalem named Joseph. His wife, Sara, was especially kind.

When Samuel heard the news that Joseph had been killed, Samuel knew his obligation was to help Sara, their son Jonathan, and the child Joseph never saw. Now he could help them again. Perhaps he could return God's grace and help this broken merchant.

Jonathan would refuse payment, but he would demand to pay for this man's care, just as his father had helped Samuel. It was a message from God. It was a chance to repay his debt to God for letting him live through that night.

As Samuel approached the inn with the cart, Jonathan recognized him instantly. Samuel smiled and reached out to give Jonathan a bear hug. Sara came outside to see what was happening and greeted Samuel warmly as well. Their affection was bonded by the knowledge they were mutual survivors who knew pain and found their way to a small measure of peace and trust.

"Jonathan, I need your help. This poor Jewish merchant was beaten and robbed on the road to Jericho. Can you help him?"

Jonathan replied, "You have our word we will do the best we can."

Jonathan and Sara turned toward the cart and saw Cassius, who starting to shake. Sara started to cry at his condition but quickly ordered the three men to lift him and take him inside.

"Jonathan," said Sara, "Quickly, send Jason to find the doctor and ask for his help!"

Samuel reached over to Jonathan and handed him a bag of denarii. "Jonathan, I owe your family so much, take this and I'll reimburse you for any extra expenses when I return. And do not refuse me; it is just part of my repayment to God for your father saving me."

Jonathan accepted the money from Samuel and understood his seriousness. He also realized this money was more than enough to help this stranger.

"You are a good soul, Samuel. You and your family have a place here as long as you are in Jerusalem."

Samuel smiled and turned to Judas. "It's time to move on to the market and then home, Judas. Peace be with you, Jonathan, Sara."

MARY

Five Days Later

"Where is he? He wouldn't leave now," Mary cried. She felt a growing panic as her dreams of happiness began to fade away. It was as though the wind was blowing away all her hopes. She thought she had found someone to love, who loved her. But now she was alone again.

Cassius must have left the orchard shortly after she had, but it had been five days since anyone had seen him in the palace. Normally his appearance was at least a daily occurrence, though they had few opportunities to talk or acknowledge each other. Quiet inquiries with the palace guards proved even more frightening. They had not seen Cassius either.

The day after their meeting, there were rumors Cassius was missing. Initially, she ignored palace rumors—she had heard so many false stories she stopped paying attention to gossip. But this time the rumors were becoming real. She couldn't believe he would leave without at least telling her he had been sent on a mission for King Herod or Pontius Pilate. She felt sure that something was wrong, very wrong.

She did the only thing she could do. Kneeling next to her cot, Mary prayed.

"My God, protect him. I know he is a gentile and a Roman. Lord, I know in my heart he is a good man, better than my own family who walked away from me and sold me to Herod. He prays daily for us both. Please guide him, protect him. Please provide him sanctuary and salvation. I know Your wisdom and Your love. You have protected those outside our race before. Please keep him safe."

Mary wiped the tears away. She loaded the tray for Herod's dinner table and started to walk the date-roasted lamb and leavened bread down the hall. A moment later, she met Joanna carrying an empty jug of wine back to the kitchen.

"Did you hear the rumors, Mary? I was in the dinner chamber when I heard Herod tell the standard to take over Centurion Cassius's duties. They say he went out for a ride and hasn't been back since. His horse came back to the gates five days ago without a trace of the centurion. They think he might have been ambushed."

Mary went pale. Joanna had seen this look before, just before Mary had a seizure. She quickly dropped the jug and grabbed the tray from Mary's hands as Mary collapsed onto the floor. Mary shook uncontrollably. Her seizure lasted for minutes. Convulsing on the floor, she finally curled herself into a fetal position, sweating and unconscious. There was blood next to her head where she hit the floor.

Joanna screamed for help. Moments later, two of Cassius's palace guards saw Mary and understood. They ordered Joanna to deliver Herod's meal and return to clean the floor while they carried Mary to her quarters.

After an hour, Mary started to regain consciousness but was still dizzy and disoriented. Joanna sat by her side, begging Mary to wake. She had never seen Mary's seizures as serious as this.

"Rest, Mary. You'll need your strength tomorrow."

Mary's face revealed her emotions. "Joanna, is he really dead? Tell me he isn't."

Joanna immediately understood Mary's distress. Joanna knew her friend loved the tall centurion. It was hard not to notice him in the palace with his polished bronze uniform and scarlet cloak.

Mary started to cry uncontrollably.

"Mary, listen. They don't know if Cassius is dead, they just assume he is. He may still be alive."

Joanna saw in Mary's face a dramatic change, and she feared she had made a mistake. Mary became still, as though she were somewhere else. Joanna reached for a cloth to dry her eyes and gently lay Mary back down on her bed.

Mary looked up. "He's alive. God would not do this. He would not bring us this far for nothing."

"Sleep, Mary. You'll feel better in the morning."

Mary closed her eyes but did not sleep. For hours she prayed, fighting her instinct to believe that Cassius was dead. Finally, sleep overtook her fears, and she entered a world of dreams.

Walking down the middle of the Bethlehem Road, Mary was searching for someone, but she didn't know who, or where to look for them. She couldn't tell which direction to go. Each step forward brought her more doubts and increased her fears. Mary started running and crying, her uncertainty adding to her growing fears. With each step, she could feel the painful pounding of her heart. She wept uncontrollably. Finally, in exhaustion, she fell to her knees and collapsed on the road.

She lay there for what seemed an eternity until the western wind increased and played through the trees as if they were strings on a harp. Mary lifted her head and looked around, finding it strange that a breeze could make the trees sing. Mary gazed toward the road and saw something she could not believe or understand. Too afraid to move, she remained lying on the ground, transfixed by the figure approaching her. The light was bright, almost blinding. But Mary couldn't look away.

The figure stopped and whispered to her, "Mary, get up. It's time for you to go. You will find what you seek if you look in your heart. Find me and you'll find what you seek."

HEROD'S PALACE

Mary awoke, surprised to find herself in Herod's palace. She had been dreaming. She turned over and slept until the dark, early hours of the morning, when a burst of light woke her. Mary leaned forward from bed to find herself alone in the dark room. No one else was there, or in the adjacent kitchen either. The rooms were completely dark. She couldn't imagine where the light had come from.

Mary rose from the cot and changed her clothes. It was time to find Cassius. Walking silently through the halls, Mary reached the gates without detection. Long ago, Cassius had helped her memorize the palace guard patrol's routines.

Outside Herod's palace, Mary began to run through the streets and alleys until she reached the outer gates. Cassius had shown Mary a secret entrance used by the guards. Mary swept past the guards unnoticed. Outside Jerusalem, she hurried down the road toward Bethlehem, knowing she had no clue where to start her search. But she decided to begin where she had last seen Cassius.

It wasn't far before Mary stopped. She looked up, afraid. The sky was clearing on a scarlet, sunlit morning.

"Please, God, help me. I'm alone. I'm afraid. I've been alone for so long and now I need to find Cassius. Please help me. Guide me. What am I going to do? Where am I going?"

At that moment, everything stood still, as if time had stopped. Birds hung in the air. Trees stopped blowing in the wind. Dropping leaves halted. A stillness consumed everything. Mary's doubts were gone. There was just the moment and the stillness. In that gap of reality came a clarity of mind Mary had never known before.

As she took her first step forward, Mary Magdalene changed. Fear melted away and determination took its place. She knew she would find Cassius, but she needed to find that man in her dreams first. He would give her answers. Only He could save them both.

As she started walking, her confidence grew, and she walked with a new purpose. Somehow, she knew she would find her answers by going home. Exhausted, Mary walked back to the palace to gather her meager possessions and travel north to Galilee.

STAFF AND SWORD INN

Cassius awoke late in the afternoon. Everything he saw was doubled, and a halo of light circled his eyes. The pressure in his head resulted in an intense headache. Vertigo set in and he immediately closed his eyes, trying to find someplace on his body that didn't hurt. He kept turning his body on the cot until he found the position of least pain. The room was dark, but from what little he could see it was a simple room. Several cots were present. From the vague image, he didn't recognize where he was or how he had gotten here. His last memories were lying beside the road after his attack. There was an image of a man who had approached him during the night, but he wasn't sure if it was a dream or real.

A woman walked into the room and softly spoke. Still groggy, Cassius couldn't understand what she was saying until she approached with a cup of warm soup.

Sara gently lifted Cassius's head and brought the soup to his lips. Though he was bruised, his ribs broken, and his face swollen, Sara was able to recognize that Cassius was not a merchant. His lack of beard and haircut indicated something else. The calluses on his hands combined with his muscled body didn't indicate a merchant or a farmer. Sara suspected he might be a Roman, perhaps a soldier.

"Can you speak?" she asked.

Cassius nodded and moaned a few words in broken Aramaic. "A little, I think. Where am I?"

"Good, though it best not to talk too much," Sara answered softly. "You are at our inn, the Staff and Sword, in Jerusalem. You were attacked on the road to Bethlehem. Do you remember anything?"

"Very little," Cassius answered and then immediately passed out.

Sara felt pity for the man, no matter his background. She prayed for his healing; no man deserved to be beaten so badly.

Knowing he was unconscious, Sara placed a hand on his chest, over his heart. "I will be back. No matter who you are, God sent you. We have a duty to heal you."

Cassius's recovery was quicker than expected, but it still took time. It was several more days before Cassius could hold a conversation. A younger man came into his room and looked at him as though he had seen him before, somewhere in the city.

"My name is Jonathan. You are healing but need time before we can move you. We had a doctor attend to you. He believes you have several broken ribs, but it's the head injuries that will take the most time to heal. Are you a Roman soldier?"

"Yes, thank you. But I need to return to my duties," replied Cassius.

"In a few days when it is safe to move you. In the meantime, rest. You are safe here. What is your name?"

"Cassius." He tried to stand but fell back onto his cot.

He knew Jonathan's face was familiar, but his mind wasn't clear enough to remember where he had seen him. Vertigo set in and he lay down again. He thought about trying to get a message to Mary but then thought better of the idea. Even if he trusted his hosts, he worried the inquiry would give away his relationship with Mary and place them both in danger. It was well understood that a common soldier who deserted his command would receive punishment, typically flogging. But a ranking centurion who betrayed his office and oath would be judged for a much more serious offense. His punishment was death.

Jonathan stared at Cassius as realization dawned. He was the officer who had saved both Matthias and him from Barabbas's attack and later saved the Jew from a soldier's beating.

"You are safe here," Jonathan said with more compassion. "We are busy finishing this inn. I hope the noise does not disturb your recovery."

"You are kind. I am in your debt." Cassius looked into Jonathan's eyes and remembered seeing him in the streets of Jerusalem.

"You are in the debt of the man who brought you here. There are good men among the Samaritans. His name is Samuel. Long ago, he helped us when my father was killed in this inn. I was a young boy, but I'll never forget his giving heart. We all owe debts," Jonathan replied. "Rest well. My mother will care for you."

Jonathan left, knowing this man was not a stranger. But there was something else he could not figure out—Cassius was a part of a distant memory he had lost in the abyss of his mind.

As Sara prepared Cassius's evening meal, Yeshua walked into the kitchen. He and James had just finished their work for the day and wanted to talk to her. The inn was almost complete, and they were busy with the finishing work, making the inn hospitable. Sara had been avoiding Yeshua and James. She knew they were getting close to leaving, and she didn't want to face the inevitable loss of these two carpenters she had learned to cherish. The older one, Yeshua, was an easy man to love.

"Sara, let me bring this meal to your guest. It would be my pleasure."

Sara looked at Yeshua and watched his hands cover her weathered grip around the bowl of vegetables. His hands were warm, soothing her tired hands. Her heart relaxed, she calmed, and a sadness stirred in her eyes.

"You work so hard for everyone, Sara. You are a blessed woman."

Sara looked at Yeshua, tears filling her eyes. "No, Yeshua. We owe you and James so much for your hard work."

Sara hesitated for a moment. "We will miss you, Yeshua. You have a special place in our hearts, especially in Jonathan's. You changed him. He's more relaxed, more kind to others. I saw the love in him before his father died. We owe you so much. This is your home, too. Please remember that."

Yeshua squeezed Sara's hands gently. Standing next to him, she felt his love penetrate the protective barriers she had built over the years. She could no longer hold back her fears, her pain. Sara started to sob uncontrollably.

As she cried, Sara released all of her pain, the loss of her husband, the years of insecurity, her loneliness, and her fear of losing Jonathan and Mara. Yeshua held onto Sara's hands, letting the pain flow from her heart, her broken soul. Finally releasing her, Yeshua looked down and saw a new woman. Instead of fear, there was kindness in her eyes. Her heart was open again.

Stepping back, Sara wiped the tears from her eyes and smiled. "What did you do?"

"I just allowed you to walk away from your pain, Sara. You're a free woman again. I will not forget this family."

Yeshua walked across the inn to the room where Cassius was recovering. As he entered, Cassius looked up and saw the man he thought he had seen on the Bethlehem Road in his waking dream. He stammered as Yeshua handed him his meal.

"Thank you. We've met before?" inquired Cassius.

"Yes, I've been watching your recovery. You kept mentioning a woman named Mary."

Cassius tried to clear his head, more confused than ever. "No, I mean before. But yes, Mary is special to me. I worry she is in danger."

"Both your journeys will be long, but do not fear, Centurion. She is safe. You will be with her again." Yeshua spoke softly, with the authority of someone who knew the truth. Looking down at Cassius, he placed his hand on Cassius's head.

"May God bless you, Cassius. We shall meet again."

Cassius looked up to speak, but Yeshua was gone. '*How did he know I am a Centurion? What did he mean by long road?*' Bewildered, he shook his head, immediately received a blinding headache, and then lost consciousness.

As his head cleared days later, Cassius began thinking about what Jonathan had said. Long ago, he had defended himself against a drunken Jew in an inn here in Jerusalem. A wave of shock swept through him. He remembered Jewish Zealots had burned the inn after the man's death, demonstrating against Roman oppression. They would have had to rebuild the tavern.

'*This is the burned inn; Jonathan was the child holding his dying father. I was the man who killed his father. I was defending myself,*' he thought, defensively. '*But the man wasn't armed,*' came the response in his mind. '*But I didn't know that. We were attacked by Zealots who killed Bracus. Nonetheless, he was unarmed,*' he argued with himself.

Cassius couldn't believe this was the same boy who had run to his father's aid so long ago. The man he had killed had been stumbling from his drunkenness. Cassius broke down, shaking, tears pouring from his hardened face. Falling on his knees, he couldn't bare the weight of his guilt.

'*His son is nursing me back to health. But I killed his father.*'

Cassius had always lit candles to his gods and prayed for bounty and good fortune. That evening, Cassius did something he had never done before. As Cassius knelt, he prayed to another god, the God the Jews called Yahweh. He called out to Mary to help him understand, to say the right words to this strange God.

'God of the Jews, please forgive me. Allow this man and his family to find the peace I have taken from them. Please forgive me. How can I be forgiven for something I did that brought such pain to their lives? Can I ever be forgiven?'

Cassius struggled with his newfound torment, avoiding speaking to anyone except to offer a meager Thank you for his meals. For the first time, Cassius understood real shame, a life-altering shame that shook the foundation of his soul. Cassius feared Mary's reaction as well, unsure if she would believe that he had acted in self-defense.

Three days later, Cassius was well enough to travel. He asked Jonathan to send someone to inform the garrison he was alive. He requested to tell them only that he was a soldier. But his heart was torn apart. He wanted to run away, to hide from the man he had become.

One truth kept staring Cassius in the face: he must face Jonathan before he left the inn. It was the moment he dreaded. Yet he was also desperate to return so he could find Mary and free her from her bondage.

The day of returning to the fortress arrived. Cassius awoke sweating, despite the coolness of the morning. His first thoughts were to run, leave the house undetected, and find his way back to the palace. But he knew he couldn't. He needed to face the truth and the torment inside that questioned the very man he had become. He needed to tell Jonathan and Sara the truth. He had killed Joseph.

Sara knocked and came in with his breakfast of porridge and dates. "Good morning, Cassius. Your recovery has been amazing. Jonathan has arranged a cart for your return to the fortress."

"Sara, I am in your debt. You've been so kind, especially considering I'm a Roman soldier. I don't know how I could ever repay you and your son."

Sara could see Cassius's anxiety. "It has been our honor, Cassius. What is bothering you?" she asked.

"Sara, I need to see you and Jonathan before I go. There's something I need to tell both of you."

"Certainly. Let's get you outside first, it's a beautiful day."

Cassius slowly stood and carefully walked outside, each step radiating pain to his ribs and legs. Outside the inn, Jason waited with a cart to take Cassius to the palace. Jonathan approached with the carpenters, Yeshua and James.

Cassius looked at Jonathan and then at Yeshua. He took a breath and started. "Jonathan, I owe you a debt I can never repay."

"Nonsense, Cassius, your debt was paid by Samuel."

"Jonathan, please, I need to finish. We've met before, long ago, when I was just a sergeant. I was in this inn the day your father died."

"What are you talking about?"

"I was here, Jonathan. I held the dagger that stole your father's life."

Jonathan stared at Cassius until recognition dawned on him. Pain shot through his body as though he'd been struck by lightning. Jonathan could barely speak.

Sara clutched her tormented face and dropped to her knees. "You stole something precious!" Sara wailed. "Can you even conceive how much pain we've suffered? How could you take that love away from us?"

Tears filled Cassius's eyes. "Sara, Jonathan, I'm so sorry. I didn't mean to. I was just defending myself." Cassius staggered backward, unable to find the words to provide comfort.

Jonathan shot back, "Do you know the pain? All these years without a father? Do you know how I've missed my father's voice, his touch? Do you know what it's like to live not knowing if your father approves of you? I miss him every day!"

Yeshua walked up to Jonathan and pulled Sara up from her knees. Holding Sara, Yeshua prayed, "Father, you are the blessed Creator and Savior of our people. Father, we pray that you grant these most humble servants peace from their pain. Lord, give us an understanding of your will.

"These are good people. Sara, our God watches over you. His love is with you, Jonathan, and Mara."

Yeshua looked at Jonathan and then at Cassius. "Cassius meant no harm to your father. Mourning the loss of his brother, he acted in haste, in defense. He is not your enemy."

Jonathan looked at Yeshua and cried out, "How can I forgive the man who killed my father?"

"Jonathan, forgiveness is not a gift for Cassius; it is *your* gift. It is one of God's greatest gifts of freedom from the bonds of vengeance. You can lift those bonds from yourself just as you lifted the bonds from Jason. God gives you this gift. But you just need to take it."

Yeshua looked at Cassius. "Forgive yourself, Cassius. You were not the cause of Bracus's death. You have much to do for God. Mary will need you."

Yeshua looked at Jason and nodded. Jason understood it was time to take Cassius back to the fortress. He walked up and wrapped his arm around the taller man. Turning Cassius around, Jason leveraged his weight to load him into the cart. Jason walked away with the donkey and cart. Cassius lay on the cart wondering how Yeshua knew about Bracus. Who was this man?

Jonathan held his mother in his arms, burying his face in her shoulder. They relived the pain of the past two decades. They shared a common but different pain, missing the man who had provided so much love in their lives. Yeshua knelt beside them and offered his own love, helping them to fight their overwhelming pain, and providing desperate relief. Yeshua's embrace offered a gift of hope, unspoken but strong.

"Jonathan, you are not responsible for your father's death. Neither was Cassius. For all these years you and Sara have feared to let Joseph go, but he's home with our Father. Joseph is at peace with Him." Yeshua put his hands on Jonathan's head as the young man sobbed uncontrollably.

Sara looked at Jonathan and saw something she had missed since Joseph had died—her son, the innocent boy who loved his family and wanted to be the man his father was. She was so proud of Jonathan.

Yeshua and James stayed with Jonathan and Sara until their pain subsided. Later that week, the two brothers from Nazareth finished their work and started the preparations to return to Galilee.

During their time helping at the inn, Jonathan had learned Yeshua was a carpenter of both wood and people. Yeshua seemed to create shapes and designs in their lives beyond Jonathan's or Sara's comprehension. There was no fault in his craftsmanship; he built solid foundations to last past their lifetime.

Jonathan knew there would be a hole in their lives when Yeshua left. He was especially concerned for his mother. Not quite comprehending, Jonathan knew he was a gift from their God.

That night, Jonathan helped to organize the Sabbath meal; the last one they would share with the carpenters from Nazareth. The table was centered in the inn and the menorah was placed on the table. As the day was closing, the sun shot spears of light through the clouds, striking the walls of the upstairs banquet room. Soon food appeared and everyone gathered around the long table.

As usual, Jonathan asked Yeshua to perform the Sabbath blessings, as had become the custom in the inn. Jonathan, Sara, Mara, Matthias, Susanna, Jason, and James sat around the table and recited the blessings as Yeshua led the Sabbath prayers.

Yeshua lit the candles and waved his arms three times toward himself to start the Sabbath.

"Hide your face from my sins and blot out all my iniquities. Create in me a clean heart, O God, and renew a right spirit within me. Cast me not away from your presence and take not your Holy Spirit from me.

"I acknowledge my sin to you, and I did not cover my iniquity; I said, 'I will confess my transgressions to the Lord,' and you forgave the iniquity of my sin," Yeshua recited from Psalms.

Yeshua continued with prayers for each one in the family, calling their names for the Lord to release the burdens of their pain. He asked God for forgiveness of the gentile Cassius and to release him from his pain and guilt.

During the Sabbath dinner, Yeshua talked about seeing people through their eyes, without hurt or pain. Then Yeshua said, "Close your eyes, quiet your minds, and release the urge to hate or seek revenge. God's love for his people stretches beyond time, beyond the heavens. Our people have betrayed our Lord so many times. Yet he still loves with the compassion of a Father and has not given up on his people. If we cannot forgive each other of our own inequities, how can our Father forgive us of our sins against his will?"

Jonathan looked at Sara and Mara and found relief. Their eyes shone with a joy he had not seen in a long time. He looked at Jason and found a new strength in a once-broken man. Finally, Jonathan looked directly into Yeshua's eyes and saw the strength in his words, in his presence.

Yeshua continued, "The road ahead for us all will be filled with rocks. Have faith that our Heavenly Father will deliver us from the bondage of this world and forgive us of our sins." He turned to Matthias and said, "Matthias, you are a good man, who has long served our Father and his people. Your reward will be great."

A thought shook Jonathan to the core: Yeshua wasn't just reciting the prayers; he was talking directly to God. He was asking God to help Jonathan and his family live these prayers, to escape the hurt of past pain and revenge. Jonathan saw a door opening in Yeshua's eyes that led to a completely new world.

The Sabbath meal was a turning point for the family. They would never view the world around them with the same eyes as before. Jonathan and Sara understood that to really live they needed to fully forgive Cassius, to let go of the pain buried inside. Yeshua brought them a special gift: forgiveness would set them free.

The next morning, well before dawn, Yeshua and James started their journey back to Nazareth. Yeshua knew his simple life as a carpenter would be short. He had appointments that had been predestined since the start of time.

EPILOGUE

Yeshua and James walked through the darkened predawn streets of Jerusalem until they reached the Fish Gate, leading them north to the road that led to Galilee. As Yeshua walked out of Jerusalem, he motioned to James to turn right and proceed up the path toward the mound overlooking Jerusalem—Golgotha. Climbing up the hill, the brothers stopped and gazed back at the sun as it illuminated the waking Jerusalem. Light rushed into the windows of city homes, robbing the inhabitants of their protective darkness, demanding that they meet the emerging day. The yellow light pierced a crimson sky as the brothers looked down upon the city.

Yeshua looked down and shivered, recognizing that they stood on the same spot where Abraham had offered Isaac as a sacrifice to God a thousand years before. Yeshua paused as he noted his similarity to Isaac. *I've always been the castaway son, like Isaac. Years of illegitimacy ridicule, the taunting looks from the people of Nazareth. Yet they still don't understand why I'm here.'*

"Yeshua, are you coming home? Mom has always been afraid you'd leave someday," said James.

"She is correct. There are other roads I must travel. And the final road I must walk alone, James. Our Heavenly Father has been waiting for me to teach this world about his forgiveness. But I still have a little time," Yeshua responded.

James looked at Yeshua, not sure how to ask the multitude of questions he had for his older brother. Instead, he just turned and looked back at Jerusalem.

James marveled at the multitude of smoke plumes from morning breakfast fires, and the steady stream of women and children walking to the city cisterns to gather water. Jerusalem was alive. As the brothers stood side by side in the morning hues, their silence struck a deeper bond between them. Their companionship was enough.

"I will come back to see Jonathan and his family again, James. We'll have one more Passover meal in the inn," Yeshua said.

Yeshua turned and put his arm around James's shoulders. "Come, we have a journey north. Do not be worried. We have time before I leave on my final journey."

Still bewildered and swallowing a lump in his throat, James could only answer with his heart. "I love you, Yeshua."

James turned and followed Yeshua down the hill, to the road leading back to Nazareth.

The adventures will continue in Book II of
the *Finding Courage* series ...

ACKNOWLEDGMENTS

Without two people, this book would have been an unfulfilled dream, forever haunting me for things I never finished. But that was not the case.

My wife, **Corinne**, who kept encouraging and prodding me to continue writing. Oddly enough, my wife didn't think I was crazy to want to write a novel. Without her support, I couldn't get very far in life.

I can't say enough good things about **Maryanna Young** from Aloha Publishing. She kept believing in me despite the rough road. And of course, correcting me when I got off the path. Patience is not just a virtue, it's a spiritual gift. I'd like to give special thanks to **Heather Goetter** of Aloha Publishing for taking my gibberish and turning it into English. I can't thank both of you enough. And to **Megan Terry** for being my first writing coach and getting me started with confidence on this project.

There's also a special thanks to **Garry Krum**, who was kind enough to point out the holes in the manuscript, helping me to tie it together when it didn't quite make sense.

ABOUT THE AUTHOR

FOSTER NASH
CODY, WYOMING

For those not familiar with Cody, it's a tourist town, just east of Yellowstone National Park. Starting in May, there's a sojourn of tourists coming through Cody to visit Yellowstone. Some stop for the daily rodeo, and most come to see the mountains and what others describe as "God's country." But mostly they come to see something different, something majestic.

Because of the tourists, the Cody population doubles in the summer. Fortunately, by the fall tourists leave and Cody settles back to the ten thousand Wyoming residents not afraid of the winter. It's a nice town. Typically, a quiet town. Traffic jams occur when deer cross the road or the occasional cattle get loose. There's a three-day Fourth of July Parade, and yes, we still have a Christmas parade. The high school football team is state champs again. They must feed them more in Cody than in other places.

Walking down the streets of Cody, sometimes I take notice of the tourists passing through and wonder what kind of life they have lived. Did they grow up in the same town most of their lives? Are they here in Cody to see something special, or are they trying to escape the lives they have back home? Do they want to be a cowboy?

I see families walking down the streets holding hands or trying to corral their kids out of the tourist shops. A lot of the kids are dragged here by their parents and can't lift their eyes away from their cell phones long enough to see the beauty of the mountains in front of them.

Please understand that it's still kind of new to me too. You see, I just moved to Cody four years ago. I didn't grow up here. I landed here by the grace of our Lord.

I've lived in twenty-three separate towns, eleven different states, and overseas. For the most part, I never chose where I lived. I followed my family when they moved and I went to school where I was accepted. As an adult, I moved where the military sent me. I got to ask for new assignments, but they still called them 'orders'.

I've had a lot of different jobs. I was a CPA for years, then in the Navy, I was Electronics Officer, Gunnery Officer, 1st Lieutenant, Logistics Officer, Pentagon Staffer, Financial Manager, Business Consultant, and EMT. I got to drive destroyers and run some fairly big financial budgets.

Later in life, I played polo and I still have my favorite polo horse, Stinky. I also learned to create glass artwork in a Westport, Massachusetts studio, then gave away most of my creations, good and bad.

I've failed previous marriages, but now I'm married to a wonderful woman who doesn't mind my quirks. I guess there's even hope for us knuckleheads. Most of all, I want my life to honor my Lord. Despite my faults, I promised Him I won't give up trying.

So, watching the people passing by in Cody, I guess I wouldn't change anything. After all, the same winding path that brought me here, also brought me to my Lord and the people I love.